致敬译界巨匠许渊冲先生

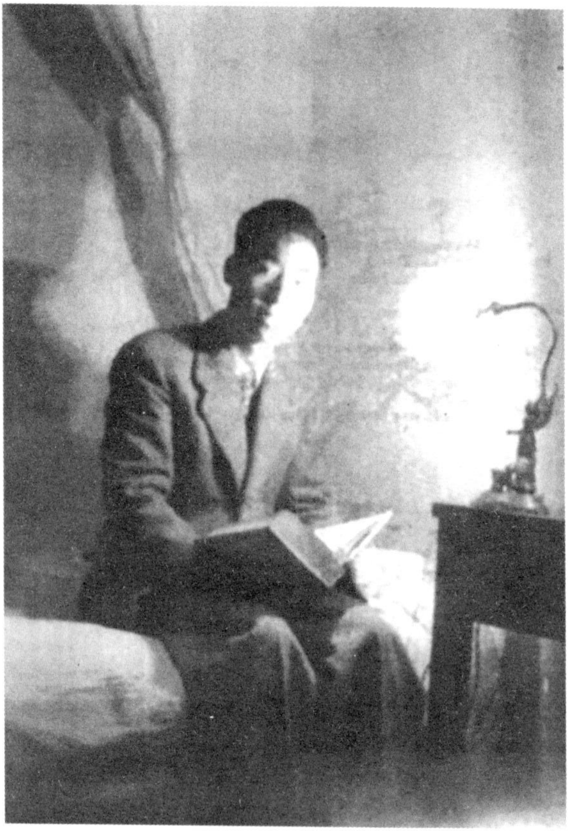

许 渊 冲 译
王 维 诗 选

SELECTED POEMS OF WANG WEI

| 编 | 译 |

中国出版集团
中译出版社

目录 Contents

| 译序
Translator's Preface

五言绝句

002　息夫人
A Captive Lady

004　孟城坳
The City Gate

006　鹿柴
The Deer Enclosure

008　栾家濑
The Rapids

010　白石滩
White-Pebbled Shallows

012　竹里馆
The Bamboo Hut

014　辛夷坞
The Magnolia Dale

016　漆园
A Petty Officer

018　鸟鸣涧
The Dale of Singing Birds

020　山中送别
Parting in the Hills

022　杂诗（三首其二）
Our Native Place (II)

024　相思
Love Seed

026 书事
Green Moss

028 山中
In the Hills

030 莲花坞
The Lotus Blooms

032 上平田
The Upland Tillers

034 萍池
The Duckweed Pool

036 华子冈
The Mountain Ridge

038 文杏馆
The Literary Hall

040 木兰柴
The Magnolia Valley

042 临湖亭
The Lakeside Pavilion

044 南垞
The Southern Shore

046 欹湖
The Slanted Lake

048 别辋川别业
Leaving My Riverside Cottage

五言律诗

050 春中田园作
Rural Spring

052 新晴野望
Field View After Rain

054 辋川闲居赠裴秀才迪
For My Outspoken Friend Pei Di in My Hermitage

056 酬张少府
For Subprefect Zhang

058 送梓州李使君
Seeing Governor Li Off to Zizhou

060 过香积寺
The Temple of Incense

062 山居秋暝
Autumn Evening in the Mountains

064 终南别业
My Hermitage in Southern Mountain

066 归嵩山作
Coming Back to Mount Song

068 终南山
Mount Eternal South

070 观猎
Hunting

072 汉江临泛
A View of the River Han

074 使至塞上
On Mission to the Frontier

076 秋夜独坐
Sitting Alone on an Autumn Night

078 李处士山居
A Scholar's Retreat

080 渡河到清河作
Crossing the Yellow River

082 酬虞部苏员外过蓝田别业不见留之作
For a Visitor Impromptu to My Blue Field

084 酬比部杨员外暮宿琴台朝跻书阁率尔见赠之作
Reply to Financier Yang on His Visit to the Lute Terrace

086 送张五归山
Seeing Zhang the Fifth Back to the Mountain

088 喜祖三至留宿
For Zu the Third Passing the Night with Me

090 冬晚对雪忆胡居士家
For a Buddhist Friend on a Snowing Night

092 归辋川作
Back to My Waterside Cottage

094 山居即事
Rural Life

096 辋川闲居
Leisurely Life by Riverside

098 春园即事
Spring in My Garden

100 淇上田园即事
My Garden by Riverside

102 晚春与严少尹与诸公见过
For Vice-Prefect Yan and Others in Late Spring

104 过感化寺昙兴上人山院
For Buddhist Tanxing in His Temple

106 郑果州相过
On Governor Zheng's Visit

108 送钱少府还蓝田
Seeing Qian Qi Off to His Blue Field

110 送杨长史赴果州
Seeing Prefect Yang Off to Guozhou

112 送邢桂州
Seeing Commissioner Xing Off

114 凉州郊外游望
A Rustic Scene on the Border

116 春日上方即事
For a Buddhist in His Cell

118 登裴迪秀才小台
On the Garden Terrace of Pei Di

120 千塔主人
For a Hermit Under the Pagoda

七言绝句

122 少年行（四首其一）
Song of Youngsters (I)

124 九月九日忆山东兄弟
Thinking of My Brothers on Mountain-Climbing Day

126 送元二使安西
A Farewell Song

128 送沈子福之江东
Seeing a Friend Off to the East

130 伊州歌
Song of Lovesickness

132 戏题盘石
Written at Random on a Rock

134 与卢员外象过崔处士兴宗林亭
Cui's Bower in the Forest

136 寒食汜上作
Cold Food Day on River Si

138 秋夜曲
Song of an Autumn Night

七言律诗

140 奉和圣制从蓬莱向兴庆阁道中留春雨中春望之作应制
Written in the Same Rhymes as His Majesty's Verse on a Spring Scene in Rain Written on His Way from the Fairy Palace to the Celebration Hall

142 和贾舍人早朝
Reply to Jia Zhi's Morning Levee

144 出塞作
Out of the Frontier

146 春日与裴迪过新昌里访吕逸人不遇
Visit to an Absent Hermit

148 积雨辋川庄作
Rainy Days in My Riverside Hermitage

150 寒食城东即事
Cold Food Day in the East of the Town

152 早秋山中作
Written in the Mountain in Early Autumn

其 他

154 陇西行
Song of the Frontier

156 送别
At Parting

158 春夜竹亭赠钱少府归蓝田
Written on a Spring Night in the Pavilion of Bamboo on Qian Qi's Return to His Blue Field

160	答张五弟	
	Reply to Cousin Zhang the Fifth	
162	渭川田家	
	Rural Scene by River Wei	
164	奉寄韦太守陟	
	For Governor Wei Zhi	
166	秋夜独坐怀内弟崔兴宗	
	Thinking of Cousin Cui on an Autumn Night	
168	过李揖宅	
	A Visit to Li Yi's Cottage	
170	送宇文太守赴宣城	
	Seeing Governor Yuwen Off to Xuancheng	
172	青溪	
	The Blue Stream	
174	送秘书晁监还日本国	
	Seeing Secretary Chao Back to Japan	
176	晓行巴峡	
	Passing Through the Gorge in the Morning	
178	西施咏	
	Song of the Beauty of the West	
180	田园乐(七首其二)	
	Seven Idylls (II)	
182	田园乐(七首其三)	
	Seven Idylls (III)	
184	田园乐(七首其四)	
	Seven Idylls (IV)	
186	田园乐(七首其五)	
	Seven Idylls (V)	
188	田园乐(七首其六)	
	Seven Idylls (VI)	

190 田园乐（七首其七）
Seven Idylls (VII)

192 陇头吟
A Frontier Song

194 桃源行
Song of Peach Blossom Land

译序

唐代(618—907)是中国诗人的黄金时代,那时中国就有了丰富多彩的各种流派的诗人,如田园诗人有王维(699—761),浪漫诗人有李白(701—762),古典诗人有杜甫(712—770),现实主义诗人有白居易(772—846),象征主义诗人有李商隐(812—858)。关于王维,宋代苏轼曾赞之曰"诗中有画,画中有诗"。诗中有画的名句是《使至塞上》中的一联:

大漠孤烟直,长河落日圆。

诗中的孤烟和画中的一样直,但在大漠的陪衬下,似乎比画中显得更直;诗中的落日和画中的一样圆,但在长河的烘托下,似乎比画中还更圆了。这就是艺术超越自然的力量。孤烟和落日都是眼睛看得见的,诗中画出似乎并不困难,困难的是要画出眼睛看不见的东西,如《送沈子福之江东》:

杨柳渡头行客稀,罟师荡桨向临圻。
惟有相思似春色,江南江北送君归。

相思是看不见的内心感情，王维却把相思比作杨柳渡头的春色，顺着南北江岸一直延伸到临圻，把友人送到江东。这就使看不见的相思充溢了江岸的空间，充满了诗人和友人的心灵，这就使诗人的画胜过画家的画了。诗人不但可以写出看不见的感情，还可以写出听不见的音乐。如《鸟鸣涧》：

> 人闲桂花落，夜静春山空。
> 月出惊山鸟，时鸣春涧中。

春天的脚步是听不见的，但是诗人却借他的耳朵给我们听，在春天桂花落地的时候，在静夜空山之中，月出惊动了山鸟，使春天的山涧中充满了春意。这山鸟的歌唱就是春天的声音，王维借鸟鸣让我们听到了春天，除了视觉、听觉之外，王维还能写出我们的感觉或触觉，如《山中》：

> 荆溪白石出，天寒红叶稀。
> 山路元无雨，空翠湿人衣。

白石和红叶可画也可写，但是空翠如何画，如何写呢？诗人把它比作看得见、听得到的雨，再加上一个摸得到的"湿"，这样视觉、听觉、触觉三官并用，就使人看到、感到翠绿的微雨点点滴滴，润湿了人的衣服，也陶醉了人的心灵，这就是天人合一了。要做到天人合一，可以读读《送春辞》：

> 日日人空老，年年春更归。
> 相欢在尊酒，不用惜花飞。

Translator's Preface

The Tang Dynasty (618-907) was the golden age of Chinese poetry, in which we had pastoral poet Wang Wei (701-761), romantic poet Li Bai (701-762), classical poet Du Fu (712-770), realistic poet Bai Juyi (772-846) and symbolic poet Li Shangyin (812-858). Wang Wei's poems, said Su Shi (1037-1101) of the Song Dynasty, are picturesque and his pictures are poetic. For example, we may read the following verse:

In boundless desert lonely smoke rises straight;
Over endless river the sun sinks round.

In these two verses we see the lonely smoke as straight and the sinking sun as round as in a picture, so we may say his verse is picturesque. As the lonely smoke and the sinking sun are visible, it is not difficult to picture them in his verse. What is more difficult is to picture the invisible. For instance, we may read his quatrain on *Seeing a Friend Off to the East*:

At willow-shaded ferry passengers are few;
Into the eastward stream the boatman puts his oars.
Only my longing heart looks like the vernal hue,
It would go with you along northern and southern shores.

How could we see a longing heart? The poet imagines it is like the vernal hue of willow shade which follows his friend on his eastern way, so he lends his mind's eye for us to see the invisible. Thus we may say his verse is more picturesque than a picture. Not only can the invisible be seen, but even the inaudible can be heard in his verse. We may read two lines from *The Dale of Singing Birds*:

> *The moonrise startles birds to sing;*
> *Their twitter fills the dale with spring.*

Spring is inaudible, but the poet lends us his ear to hear the song of spring in the twitter of the birds. So we may say the poet has ears as sharp as his eyes. What is more, his verse can make us feel the intangible. For instance, we may read the following couplet from *In the Hills*:

> *Along the path no rain is seen,*
> *My gown is moist with drizzling green.*

The green is visible but not audible nor tangible, but

the poet makes us hear the color drizzle like rain and feel it moisten the gown. So we may say his poetry is visible, audible and tangible for in his verse we can see, hear and feel his communion with nature, which is his way of living. To end our Foreword, I'll cite his quatrain *Farewell to Spring*:

> *From day to day man will grow old;*
> *Spring will come back from year to year.*
> *Enjoy the cup of wine you hold!*
> *Grieve not over flowers fallen here!*

许渊冲译王维诗选

息夫人

莫以今时宠,
能忘旧日恩。
看花①满眼泪,
不共②楚王言。

① 看花:此处代指富裕的享乐生活。
② 共:与,和。

息夫人本是春秋时息国君主之妻,后为楚王所掳。她虽在楚生了两个孩子,但始终没有和楚王说过一句话。诗的前两句拟息夫人口吻:不要以为你今天的宠爱,就能使我忘掉旧日的恩情。突出了旧恩的珍贵难忘,显示了淫威和富贵并不能征服弱者的心灵,而所谓的新宠实际上是一种侮辱。诗的后两句则是说息夫人在富丽华美的楚宫里,看着本来使人愉悦的花朵,却是满眼泪水,对在她身边的楚王始终不共一言。这沉默越发彰显了息夫人蓄积在心底的对楚王的灭国毁家之恨。诗人塑造了一个身受屈辱,但在沉默中反抗的妇女形象。

A Captive Lady

Think not the royal favor of these years
Could efface her love for the vanquished king.
The sight of flowers fills her eyes with tears,
She won't tell the conqueror anything.

孟城坳[1]

[1] 坳(ào): 有低洼的地方。

新家[2]孟城口,
古木余衰柳。
来者[3]复为谁?
空悲昔人有。

[2] 家: 住到。

[3] 来者: 以后来的人。

此诗是《辋川集》里的第一首。诗人新近搬到孟城口。孟城口本是初唐诗人宋之问的别墅,而可叹的是,如今那里只有疏落的古木和枯萎的柳树,呈现出一片衰败凋零的景象。此时,正值李林甫擅权,张九龄罢相,王维隐退辋川。当他看到这一衰败景象时,无法抑制忧闷的心情:如今我为"昔人"而悲,以后的"来者"是否又会为我而悲呢?

The City Gate

I've moved in near the city gate
Where withered willow trees are left.
Should another move here too late,
Alas! Of trees he'd be bereft.

鹿　柴[①]

[①] 鹿柴(zhài)：王维辋川别墅之一。柴，通"砦"或"寨"，用树木围成的栅栏。

空山不见人，
但闻人语响。
返景[②]入深林，
复照青苔上。

[②] 返景(yǐng)：同"返影"，太阳即将落山时，通过云反射的阳光。

许渊冲译王维诗选

　　这首诗是王维后期山水诗的代表作。王维是诗人、画家兼音乐家。这首诗正体现出诗、画、乐的结合。无声的静寂、无光的幽暗，一般人都易于觉察；但有声的静寂，有光的幽暗，则较少为人所注意。诗人正是以他画家、音乐家对色彩、声音特有的敏感，才把握住了空山人语响和返照入深林那一刹那间所显示的特有的幽静境界。而这种敏感，又是和诗人的称号"诗佛"相关，即诗人不仅在用眼睛去细致观察大自然，更在潜心去默会这个世界。

The Deer Enclosure

In pathless hills no man's in sight,
But I still hear echoing sound.
In gloomy forest peeps no light,
But sunbeams slant on mossy ground.

栾家濑[①]

[①] 濑（lài）：石沙滩上水流湍急的地方。

飒飒[②]秋雨中，
浅浅[③]石溜[④]泻。
跳波[⑤]自相溅，
白鹭惊复下。

[②] 飒（sà）飒：风雨的声音。

[③] 浅（jiān）浅：水流的声音，形容水流很急。

[④] 石溜（liù）：经过石头上方的急促水流。

[⑤] 跳波：跳跃的波浪。

这首小诗描写了这样一个有趣的情景：山谷中有一浅濑，一只鹭鸶正在全神贯注地觅食，突然"飒飒秋雨"使得急流猛然与坚石相击，溅起的水珠打在鹭鸶身上，吓得它展翅惊飞。而当鹭鸶明白这是一场虚惊之后，便又安详地飞了下来，落在原处。诗人巧妙地以宁中有惊、以惊见宁的艺术手法，通过"白鹭惊复下"的一场虚惊来反衬栾家濑的安宁和静穆。在这里，没有任何潜在的威胁，可以过着无忧无虑的宁静生活，这正是此时走出政治旋涡的诗人所追求的理想境界。

The Rapids

In rustling autumn rain
Water on pebbles dashes,
And starts the egret when
It sprinkles into splashes.

白 石 滩

清浅白石滩,
绿蒲①向②堪③把。
家住水东西,
浣④纱明月下。

① 蒲:一种水生草本植物。

② 向:将近,差不多。

③ 堪:可以,能够。

④ 浣(huàn):洗。

  白石滩是辋水边上由一片白石形成的浅滩,是著名的辋川二十景之一。王维的山水诗非常注意表现景物的光线和色彩,这首诗就是用暗示的手法写月夜的光线。月之明,水之清,蒲之绿,石之白,相映相衬,给人造成了极其鲜明的视觉感受。本诗的前两句是静态的景物描写,后两句则给白石滩添上了众多鲜活的浣纱少女形象,使得整个画面充满了生气。

White-Pebbled Shallows

Water is clear and pebbles white,

Green reeds can be counted in moonlight.

Maidens east and west of the streams

All wash their silks by the moonbeams.

竹 里 馆

独坐幽篁①里,
弹琴复长啸②。
深林人不知,
明月来相照。

① 篁:竹林。
② 长啸(xiào):撮口而呼,类似打口哨,这里指吟咏、歌唱。古代一些超逸之士常用来抒发感情。

诗中写到景物,只用六个字:"幽篁""深林""明月"。诗中写人物活动,也只用六个字:"独坐""弹琴""长啸"。表面看来,四句诗的用字造句平淡无奇,但整体看这首小诗,却妙谛自成,境界自出,蕴含着一种特殊的艺术魅力。本诗也是《辋川集》中的一首名作,它的妙处在于所显示的是一个令人自然而然为之吸引的意境,不以字句取胜,而从整体见美。它的美在神不在貌,而其神是蕴含在意境之中的。

The Bamboo Hut

Sitting among bamboos alone,
I play my lute and croon carefree.
In the deep woods where I'm unknown,
Only the bright moon peeps at me.

辛夷坞[1]

① 坞:中央低四周高的谷地。

木末芙蓉花[2],
山中发红萼[3]。
涧户[4]寂无人,
纷纷开且落。

② 木末芙蓉花:指辛夷花因辛夷花颜色与形态与莲花相近,莲花又名芙蓉,而辛夷花开在树梢,故以"木末芙蓉花"借指。木末:树梢。
③ 萼(è):花萼,花开时托着花瓣的部分。
④ 涧户:涧口,山溪口。

辛夷花的花苞结在每一根枝条的最末端,形如毛笔,所以诗歌用了"木末"二字来形容。辛夷含苞待放时,很像荷花箭,花瓣和颜色也近似之,因而称为"芙蓉"。春来到人间,辛夷欣欣然地绽开神秘的蓓蕾,是那样灿烂,好似云蒸霞蔚。而有花开就有花落,这山中的红萼,点缀着寂寞的涧户,最后又纷纷扬扬地向人间撒下片片落英。这首五绝,在描绘了辛夷花给静寂的山涧带来美好、繁华的同时,又写出了人间的一种落寞。

The Magnolia Dale

The magnolia-tipped trees
In mountains burst in flowers.
The mute brook-side house sees
Them blow and fall in showers.

漆　园

古人①非傲吏，
自阙②经世务③。
偶寄④一微官，
婆娑数株树。

① 古人：这里指庄子。

② 阙（quē）：欠缺。

③ 经世务：经国济世的能力。

④ 寄：寄身于。

漆园亦是辋川二十景之一，不过本诗着眼于与漆园有关的典故而非景物。《史记》载，庄子曾为漆园吏，楚威王遣使聘他为相，庄子却说："子亟去，无污我！"因为庄子啸傲王侯的故事，郭璞在《游仙诗·其一》中称庄子为"漆园有傲吏"。王维反其意而用之，借古人自喻，表明自己隐居而绝无傲世之意，做个漆园吏，正好可借漆园隐逸，以"婆娑数株树"为伴，从而表明诗人隐逸恬退的生活情趣和自甘淡泊的人生态度。

A Petty Officer

A petty officer could not be proud,

He cannot do important jobs with ease.

Rendering service like a floating cloud,

He brings fresh showers for the thirsting trees.

鸟 鸣 涧

人闲①桂花落,
夜静春山空。
月出惊山鸟,
时②鸣春涧中。

① 闲:安静,闲适。

② 时:偶尔。

　　王维的山水诗,偏好于创造静谧的意境,而静谧体现在这首诗中却是"花落""月出""鸟鸣"这些动态的景物描写。这样的描述既使诗显得富有生机而不枯寂,同时又更加突出了春涧的幽静,这正是"鸟鸣山更幽"所蕴含的艺术辩证法的体现。在这春山中,万籁都陶醉在夜的色调与宁静中了,当月亮升起,给这夜幕笼罩的空谷带来皎洁银辉的时候,竟使山鸟惊觉起来。但可以想象,明亮的月光,却给幽谷夜的宁静带来了新的境界与意味。

The Dale of Singing Birds

Sweet laurel blooms fall unenjoyed;

Vague hills dissolve into night void.

The moonrise startles birds to sing;

Their twitter fills the dale with spring.

山中送别

山中相送罢,
日暮掩①柴扉②。
春草明年③绿,
王孙④归不归?

① 掩:关闭。
② 扉:门。
③ 明年:又作"年年"。
④ 王孙:贵族的子孙,在此处代指朋友。

这首诗写送别友人,构思却独具匠心,其最显著的特点是并非着眼于离亭饯别的依依不舍,而以"送罢"落笔,进一步着墨于送别后回家寂寞之情更浓更稠,表达了诗中人冀望于来年春草再绿之时,能与友人团聚的情怀。"春草明年绿,王孙归不归"从《楚辞·招隐士》"王孙游兮不归,春草生兮萋萋"句化来。但原句是因游子久去而叹其不归,而本诗的这两句则在与友人分别的当天就提出,更表达了与友人情谊的深厚。

Parting in the Hills

I see off the hills my compeer;

At dusk I close my wicket door.

When grass turns green in spring next year,

Will my friend come with spring once more?

杂 诗

（三首其二）

君自故乡来，
应知故乡事。
来日①绮窗②前，
寒梅③著花④未？

① 来日：来的时候。
② 绮窗：雕刻着花纹的窗户。
③ 寒梅：冬天开放的梅花。
④ 著（zhuó）花：开花。

　　本诗开篇就以一种不加修饰，近似讲话的语气表达诗中人急于向故乡人了解故乡事的心情。而关于故乡事，诗中人独问的却是："来日绮窗前，寒梅著花未？"仿佛故乡值得怀念的就是窗前那株寒梅。这窗前的寒梅可能蕴含着当年家居生活亲切有趣的情事。因此，这株寒梅就成了故乡的一种象征，被诗化和标志化了，自然也成了诗中人思乡之情的集中寄托。古代诗歌中常有这种质朴平淡而诗味浓郁的作品，它质朴到似乎不用任何技巧，实际上却包含着最高级的技巧。

Our Native Place

(II)

You come from native place;

What happened there you'd know.

Did mume blossoms in face

Of my gauze window blow?

相　思

红豆生南国，

春来发几枝？

愿君多采撷①，

此物最相思②。

① 采撷（xié）：采摘。

② 此物最相思：它最能寄托想念的情感。

本篇堪称名篇中的名篇，脍炙人口，经乐工谱曲而广为流传，是梨园弟子最爱的歌词之一。据说安史之乱后，李龟年流落江南，经常为人演唱，听者无不动容。传说古代有一位女子，因丈夫死在边塞，哭于树下而死，化为红豆，于是人们又称红豆为"相思子"。这种"相思"却不限于男女情爱，朋友之间也有相思的。此诗题一作《江上赠李龟年》，可见诗中抒写的是眷念朋友的情思。全诗句句不离红豆，"超以象外，得其圜中"，把相思之情表达得入木三分。

Love Seed

The red beans grow in Southern land.
How many load in spring the trees?
Gather them till full is your hand;
They would revive fond memories.

书 事

轻阴①阁②小雨，
深院昼慵③开。
坐看苍苔色，
欲上人衣来。

① 轻阴：微微的阴天。
② 阁：同"搁"，阻止，停止。
③ 慵（yōng）：懒得。

这是一首即事写景之作，所以题为"书事"。小雨初歇，天色尚还微阴，仿佛是轻阴迫使小雨停止，此处用笔别有趣味。这时诗人缓步走向深院，虽已是白昼，却还懒得去开那院门。淡淡两句，通过一种疏懒的情调把读者带进一片宁静的小天地。雨后的青苔，鲜绿、清新，充满生机，竟让诗人产生一种幻觉，仿佛"欲上人衣来"。这一神来之笔，展现了诗人好静的个性，与深院小景浑然交融，创造了一个物我相生、宁静而又充满生命活力的意境。

Green Moss

Light rain dissolves in gloom;
In closed yard shadows loom.
Sitting by mossy side,
I feel my robe green-dyed.

山 中

荆溪白石出,
天寒红叶稀。
山路元①无雨,
空翠②湿人衣。

① 元:原,原来。
② 空翠:指山间青色潮湿的雾气。

这幅由白石磷磷的小溪、鲜艳的红叶和无边的浓翠所组成的山中冬景,色泽斑斓鲜明,富于诗情画意,毫无萧瑟枯寂的情调。首句写天寒水浅,山溪变成涓涓细流,露出磷磷白石。次句写入冬天寒,红叶变得稀少,但是在一片浓翠的山色背景上仍然很是显眼。最后两句则写林荫覆盖的山路上虽然没有下雨,但是浓翠的树林所积聚的雾气也足以沾湿游人的衣衫。

In the Hills

White pebbles feel a blue stream glide;
Red leaves are strewn on cold hillside.
Along the path no rain is seen,
My gown is moist with drizzling green.

莲花坞[1]

[1] 坞(wù)：周围高而中间低的地方。

日日采莲去，
洲[2]长多[3]暮归。
弄[4]篙莫溅水，
畏湿红莲衣[5]。

[2] 洲：水中陆地。

[3] 多：常常。

[4] 弄：这里指撑篙。

[5] 红莲衣：红莲花色的衣服，此处指采莲女的服装。

　　这首诗是王维题友人所居的《皇甫岳云溪杂题五首》之第二首，诗歌主要咏写对荷花的喜爱，却不正面用笔。采莲人日日早出晚归，十分辛苦地采莲劳作。然而采莲人也自有他们的生活乐趣。"弄篙莫溅水，畏湿红莲衣"形象生动地展现了采莲人对莲花的珍爱与怜惜，同时也表明他们热爱生活、珍惜美好事物的情操。畏湿是担心被水溅湿的意思。

The Lotus Blooms

You go to gather lotus blooms from day to day,
And often come back late for long, long is the way.
Don't splash when you put into water your pole,
Water splashed on their rosy dress will spoil the whole.

上平田[①]

[①] 上平田：耕田。

朝耕上平田,
暮耕上平田。
借问问津者,
宁知沮溺[②]贤?

[②] 沮溺：长沮、桀溺，是两位隐者的名字。

这首诗是《皇甫岳云溪杂题五首》之第四首。沮溺，即长沮、桀溺。本首诗歌借用了《论语》中的典故。长沮、桀溺二人一起耕地劳作，孔子路过看见了他们，便让子路问津（渡口）。长沮、桀溺是避世的隐者，此处以二人喻皇甫岳，言世人不知其贤能。

The Upland Tillers

They till the upland fields by day;
They till the upland fields till night.
If you want to ask them the way,
Do you not know they are sages bright?

萍　池

春池深且广，
会①待②轻舟回。
靡靡③绿萍合，
垂杨扫复开。

① 会：应当。
② 待：须。
③ 靡靡：迟缓的，慢的。

这首诗是《皇甫岳云溪杂题五首》之第五首。一池萍水，一株垂杨，本来平淡无奇，诗人却写得何等风趣，本来是静景，却处处在动，而愈是动，愈见其静。在这里，人、舟、水、萍、杨柳、春风和谐亲近地生活在一起，王维的山水田园诗展现了人与自然的亲密和谐美，这也正是王维诗歌的一大特色。

The Duckweed Pool

The pool seems deep and wide in spring day,
When the boat is on its backward way.
Green duckweeds part and meet with ease,
When they are caressed by willow trees.

华子冈

飞鸟去不穷,
连山复秋色。
上下华子冈,
惆怅情何极!

这首诗是王维《辋川集》中的第二首,其于无限、深邃、悠远的时空中,探寻心灵的境界。秋天的黄昏,诗人在华子冈上下徘徊,遥望悠远的天空,一群群飞鸟飞向无边的天际,群山绵延,秋叶飘落,那"鸟之飞""叶之落""山之延",正是诗人的情怀,深邃而悠远,渺小而无助。

The Mountain Ridge

Birds on birds fly far, far away;
Hills on hills lost in autumn hue.
Go up and down the mountain way.
How much will you regret and rue!

文 杏①馆

① 文杏:银杏,又称白果。

文杏裁为梁,
香茅结为宇。
不知栋里云,
去作人间雨。

这是一首禅诗,诗意颇值得玩味。文杏、香茅都是名贵珍稀之物,用作"梁""宇"等建筑材料,当然是一种超凡脱俗的理想境界,而"栋里云"化作"人间雨",更是佛意的象征。全诗的艺术构思都是象征化的。诗中洋溢着释情佛意,却没有一句释言佛语,这即是象征的妙用。

The Literary Hall

The beam made of apricot tree,
The roof made of thatch and bamboo.
Rain falls when clouds on the beam flee,
To welcome happy rendezvous.

木兰①柴

① 木兰：落叶乔木。

秋山敛余照②，
飞鸟逐前侣。
彩翠③时分明，
夕岚④无处所。

② 敛余照：收敛了落日的余晖。

③ 彩翠：色彩鲜艳的翠绿的山中风光。

④ 夕岚：傍晚时山林中的雾气。

　　这首五绝，描写了傍晚时分的天色，活画出一幅秋山暮霭鸟归图。王维在观照景物时，特别注意对景物的光与色的捕捉。秋日的山顶衔着半轮残阳，很快只留下一抹余晖。晚霞把金光涂抹在每一片树叶上，是那么闪耀而鲜亮，展露着秋日山林的斑斓与艳丽。在夕照中，倦飞的鸟儿鼓动着翠羽，鸣叫着互相追逐，遁入山林，消失在飘忽不定的傍晚山林的雾气之中。

The Magnolia Valley

Autumn hills steeped in sinking sunlight,
Birds fly in chase of their dear mates.
The mountain green's now dark now bright,
Even vapor evaporates.

临湖亭

轻舸①迎上客②,
悠悠湖上来。
当③轩④对樽酒,
四面芙蓉⑤开。

① 舸(gě):小船。
② 上客:尊贵的客人。
③ 当:对着。
④ 轩:窗户。
⑤ 芙蓉:此指荷花,即水芙蓉。

诗人正在亭子里等待迎接客人,轻舸在湖上悠然驶来。宾主围坐临湖亭开怀畅饮,窗外就是一片盛开的莲花。这是何等美妙的人生境界!诗歌将美景、鲜花、醇酒和闲情巧妙地融为一体,在自然中寄深意,于质朴中见情趣,娟秀飘逸的意境,令人陶醉。

The Lakeside Pavilion

My boat goes to welcome my guest,
Slowly we sail on the calm lake.
We drink north and south, east and west,
Where lotus blooms smile for our sake.

南 垞[①]

[①] 垞(chá)：小土丘。

轻舟南垞去，
北垞淼难即[②]。　　[②] 即：到达。
隔浦[③]望人家，　　[③] 浦：湖水。
遥遥不相识。

诗人不直面南垞之景，却去写船上所见之北垞：那里三五人家，掩映于波光林霭之间，而一水盈盈相隔，可望而不可即。写得渺漫辽远，仿佛缥缈难寻的仙山圣域。其实此地水阔山高，正如诗人所愿，心中自然块垒皆消，连诗句也疏朗广漠起来。

The Southern Shore

My light boat goes to Southern shore
And leaves the Northern far away.
Looking back, I see nothing more
Than an unknown land misty gray.

欹 湖

吹箫凌①极浦②,
日暮送夫君③。
湖上一回首,
山青卷④白云。

① 凌:渡过,越过。
② 极浦:远处的水边。
③ 夫君:作者的朋友。
④ 卷:(白云)松散的样子。

　　船儿载着箫声越过长长的水边,日暮了要给行人道别。行者湖上回头再看,只见青山上舒卷着白云。箫声如诉,日暮催人,湖上回首,山静云飞,无一字说及人情,而离情已深蕴其中。这里的人间聚散,似乎也被作者看成了一道赏心悦目的风景。

The Slanted Lake

She plays on flute as far as waterside

To see her lord off with fading twilight.

He turns to look back from the lake so wide,

But finds hill on hill green, cloud on cloud white.

别辋川别业[①]

[①] 别业：别墅。

依迟[②]动车马，
惆怅出松萝。
忍别青山去，
其如绿水何！

[②] 依迟：不舍的样子。

题中所提到的别业即是开元末年购得的蓝田宋之问别墅，位于辋川谷口。乾元元年（758），王维不得不回京城长安而告别辋川，诗中充满了依依不舍的浓情。诗的大意是：我缓缓催动车马，离开长满松萝的山林，是那样依依不舍，内心充满了留恋的惆怅之情。就算我勉强含悲地离开青青的山林，却又怎能割舍这潺潺的绿水呢？这首小诗"语浅情深"，作者选取了"青山""绿水""松萝"这些典型的景物，而这些都倾注了作者全部的感情和理想，所以能够用本色语言传递真切的感受。

Leaving My Riverside Cottage

How can I drive my horse which whines
To leave my cot with pines and vines!
How can I leave my mountain screen
And my river emerald green!

春中①田园作

① 春中：仲春，农历二月。

屋上春鸠②鸣，
村边杏花白。
持斧伐远扬③，
荷锄觇④泉脉⑤。
归燕识故巢，
旧人看新历⑥。
临觞⑦忽不御⑧，
惆怅思远客。

② 春鸠（jiū）：鸟名。

③ 远扬：又长又高的桑树枝。

④ 觇（chān）：探测。

⑤ 泉脉：地下泉水的流向。

⑥ 看新历：开始新的一年。

⑦ 觞（shāng）：古人饮酒用的器皿。

⑧ 御：饮，喝。

《春中田园作》是一首春天的颂歌。本诗描绘出了春天的欣欣向荣和农民的愉快欢欣，展现了唐代前期社会的安定以及人民忙碌于生产生活的精神面貌。首联写景，鸠鸣、花白，有声有色，春意盎然。颔联写农事，农民们伐远扬、觇泉脉，既紧张又兴奋。整桑理水是经冬以后最早的一种劳动，可说是农事的序幕。颈联、尾联则表达远行者对乡土的眷恋。全诗春天的气息浓重，而诗人始终没有通过常规的万紫千红来渲染春天，而是从淡淡的色调和平静的活动中成功地表现了春天的到来。

Rural Spring

Turtledoves cooing on the height,
With apricots the village's white.
Mulberries pruned far on the mountain,
And water sourced near by the fountain.
Swallows return to their old beams;
A new almanac brings new dreams.
Can I drink alone, cup in hand?
I think of you in far-off land.

新晴①野望

① 新晴：初晴。

新晴原野旷，
极目②无氛③垢④。
郭⑤门临渡头，
村树连溪口。
白水明田外，
碧峰出山后。
农月无闲人，
倾家事⑥南亩。

② 极目：穷尽目力向远处眺望。

③ 氛：雾气，云气。

④ 垢：污秽。

⑤ 郭：外城。

⑥ 事：从事。

    诗的首联，总述雨后初晴时的感受：经过雨水的洗刷，天空蔚蓝、原野空旷，一切是那么明净新鲜，没有一点尘埃。诗人一下子就抓住了环境的特征。颔联、颈联描绘的是纵目远眺所看到的秀丽景色：田野外面，因为雨后水涨，河水泛起粼粼波光，晴日辉映，比平时显得明亮；山脊背后，一重重青翠的峰峦突兀而出，远近相衬，比平时更富于层次感。这一组风景，紧紧扣住了雨后新晴的景物特点。尾联为这幅静态画面加上了动态的人物，给原野增添了无限生机，能让人想见初夏田间活跃的情状并感受到农忙劳动的气氛。这样一笔，整个画面都活起来了。

Field View After Rain

After the rain vast looks the plain;
As far as I see, there's no stain.
The gate stands by the riverside,
The village trees spread far and wide.
Beyond the fields ripples the stream;
Behind green hills with smiles peaks beam.
In summer no peasant's at leisure,
All farmhands are busy with pleasure.

辋川闲居赠裴秀才迪

寒山转苍翠①,
秋水日潺湲②。
倚杖柴门外,
临风听暮蝉。
渡头余③落日,
墟里④上孤烟。
复值接舆⑤醉,
狂歌五柳⑥前。

① 转苍翠:也作"积苍翠"。
② 潺湲(yuán):流水声。此处形容水流缓慢。
③ 余:也作"馀"。
④ 墟里:村落,村庄。
⑤ 接舆:陆通先生的字,在这里以接舆比裴迪。
⑥ 五柳:代指陶渊明。

　　这是一首诗、画、音乐完美结合的五律。辋川在今陕西省蓝田县南终南山下,山麓有宋之问的别墅,后归王维。王维在那里住了30多年,直至晚年。诗人裴迪是王维的好友,与王维唱和较多。首联和颈联写山水原野的深秋晚景,诗人选择富有季节和时间特征的景物:苍翠的寒山、缓缓的秋水、渡口的夕阳、墟里的炊烟,有声有色,动静结合,勾勒出一幅和谐幽静而又富有生机的田园山水画。诗的颔联和尾联写诗人与裴迪的闲居之乐。倚杖柴门,临风听蝉,把诗人安逸的神态、超然物外的情致,写得栩栩如生;醉酒狂歌,则把裴迪的狂士风度表现得淋漓尽致。

For My Outspoken Friend Pei Di in My Hermitage

Cold mountains turn into deepening green;

Each day the autumn stream ripples with ease.

Out of my wicket gate on my staff I lean

To hear cicadas sing in evening breeze.

The setting sun beyond the ferry half sunk,

The village smoke rises lonely and straight.

What joy to see my outspoken friend drunk,

Chanting to five willows before my gate!

酬①张少府

① 酬：以诗词酬答。

晚年惟好静，
万事不关心。
自顾②无长策，
空知返旧林。
松风吹解带③，
山月照弹琴。
君问穷④通⑤理，
渔歌⑥入浦深。

② 自顾：自念。

③ 解带：表示闲适，不拘束。

④ 穷：不能当官。
⑤ 通：能当官。
⑥ 渔歌：隐士之歌。

《酬张少府》是诗人酬答友人的作品。题目冠以"酬"字，当是张少府先有诗相赠，王维再写此诗为酬。首联、颔联写出了诗人伟大抱负不能实现的矛盾苦闷心情。颈联写隐逸生活的情趣。尾联是即景悟情，回到题目上来，用一问一答的形式，照应了"酬"字；同时，又妙在以不答作答，可谓"韵外之致""味外之旨"。全诗着意自述"好静"之志趣，写自己对闲适生活的快意，并表示自己对天地间的大道理有所领悟，已经能超然物外。

For Subprefect Zhang

I love to be tranquil while old,
Of world affairs my mind carefree.
For long I've nothing to withhold,
I know but to lean on my tree.
My sleeves in wind caress the pine;
I play lute and let the moon peep.
As to rise and fall, rain or shine,
Hear fishing songs waft far and deep!

送梓州李使君

万壑树参天,
千山响杜鹃。
山中一夜雨①,
树杪②百重泉。
汉女输橦布③,
巴人讼芋田。
文翁翻④教授,
敢不倚先贤。

① 一夜雨:也作"一半雨"。

② 树杪(miǎo):树梢。

③ 橦(tóng)布:梓州特产,由橦木花织成的布。

④ 翻:通"反",转变成。

《送梓州李使君》是诗人为送李使君入蜀赴任而创作的一首诗。赠别之作,多从眼前景物写起,即景生情,抒发惜别之意。王维此诗,立意则不在惜别,而在劝勉,因而一上来就从悬想着笔,遥写李使君赴任之地梓州的自然风光,形象逼真,气韵生动,令人神往。诗中没有一句涉及送别之时、之地、之情、之事,全篇都是描绘巴蜀的山水、风情和民事。然而读后深思,就会发觉此诗紧紧围绕李氏即将赴任的梓州步步展开,层层深入,全诗融注着诗人对李氏欣羡、期望、劝勉的一腔真情,前后融会贯通,结构谨严缜密。全诗没有一般送别诗的感伤气氛,情绪积极开朗,格调高远明快,是唐诗中写送别的名篇之一。

Seeing Governor Li Off to Zizhou

The trees in your valley scrape the sky,

You'll hear in your hills cuckoos cry.

If it rained at night in your mountain,

You'd see your tree tips hang like fountain.

Your women weave to make a suit,

You'd try to solve people's dispute.

The sage before you opened schools,

Like him you should carry out rules.

过^①香积寺

①过:到访。

不知香积寺,
数里入云峰。
古木无人径,
深山何处钟?
泉声咽^②危^③石,
日色冷^④青松。
薄暮空潭曲^⑤,
安禅^⑥制毒龙^⑦。

②咽:发出呜咽的声音。

③危:高耸的。

④冷:为……所冷。

⑤曲:水边。

⑥安禅:此处指佛家思想。

⑦毒龙:此处指人的邪念妄想。

诗题《过香积寺》的"过",意为"访问、探望"。诗意在写山寺,但并不正面描摹,而侧写周围景物,来烘托映衬山寺之幽胜。全诗不写寺院,而寺院已在其中。最后看到深潭已空,想到佛经中所说的其性暴烈的毒龙已经制服,喻指只有克服邪念妄想,才能悟到禅理的高深,领略宁静之幽趣。这首诗构思奇妙、炼字精巧,颈联"泉声咽危石,日色

The Temple of Incense

Where is the temple? I don't know.

Miles up to Cloudy Peak I go.

There's pathless forest in the dell,

Where deep in mountain rings the bell?

The rockside fountain seems to freeze;

Sunlight can't warm up green pine trees.

I sit in twilight by the pool,

To curb my desire I'd be cool.

冷青松",历来被誉为炼字典范。"咽"字形容水声之细,"冷"字形容环境之幽,极具感情色彩。诗人用"冷"来形容日色,粗看极谬,仔细玩味,这个"冷"字实在太妙。夕阳西下,昏黄的余晖涂抹在一片幽深的松林上,这情状似曾相识,不可谓不"冷"。

山居秋暝①

① 暝（míng）：日落时分。

空山新②雨后，
天气晚来秋。
明月松间照，
清泉石上流。
竹喧③归浣女，
莲动下渔舟。
随意④春芳歇⑤，
王孙⑥自可留。

② 新：刚刚。

③ 喧：喧哗，此处指竹叶发出声响。

④ 随意：任凭。

⑤ 歇：消失，消歇。

⑥ 王孙：此处泛指隐居的人。

《山居秋暝》是王维的山水名篇，于诗情画意之中寄托着诗人高洁的情怀和对理想境界的追求。本诗的重要艺术手法是以自然美来表现诗人的人格美和一种理想中的社会之美。全诗将空山雨后的秋凉、松间明月的光照、石上清泉的声音以及浣女归来竹林中的喧笑声，渔船穿过荷花的动态，和谐完美地融合在一起，给人一种丰富新鲜的感受。本诗像一幅清新秀丽的山水画，又像一支恬静优美的抒情乐曲，体现了王维"诗中有画"的创作特点。

Autumn Evening in the Mountains

After fresh rain in mountains bare

Autumn permeates evening air.

Among pine-trees bright moonbeams peer;

O'er crystal stones flows water clear.

Bamboos whisper of washer-maids;

Lotus stirs when fishing boat wades.

Though fragrant spring may pass away,

Still here's the place for you to stay.

终南别业

中岁①颇好道②,
晚家③南山陲④。
兴来每独往,
胜事空自知。
行到水穷处,
坐看云起时。
偶然值⑤林叟⑥,
谈笑无还期。

① 中岁：中年。
② 道：此处指佛教。
③ 家：安家。
④ 陲（chuí）：边缘，此处指南山脚。
⑤ 值：碰到。
⑥ 叟（sǒu）：老翁。

这首《终南别业》是王维山水田园诗的代表作。诗人把退隐后自得其乐的闲适情趣写得有声有色，惟妙惟肖。"行到水穷处，坐看云起时"是流传千古的名句。诗人兴致来了就独自信步漫游，走到水的尽头，坐看行云变幻，这生动地刻画了一位隐者的形象，如见其人。同山间老人谈谈笑笑，把回家的时间也忘了，十分自由惬意，这是诗人捕捉到了典型环境中的典型事例，突出地表现了退隐者豁达的性格。诗语平白如话，却极具功力，诗味、理趣二者兼备。

My Hermitage in Southern Mountain

Following divine law after my middle age,
I live in Southern Mountain at my hermitage.
In joyful mood to wander, alone I would go
To find delightful scenes nobody else could know.
I'd go as far as the end of a stream or fountain
And sit and gaze on cloud rising over the mountain.
If I happen to meet with an old forest man,
We'd chat and laugh endlessly, as long as we can.

归嵩山作

清川^①带^②长薄^③,
车马去闲闲。
流水如有意,
暮禽相与还。
荒城临古渡,
落日满秋山。
迢递^④嵩高下,
归来且^⑤闭关。

① 川:河流。
② 带:环绕。
③ 薄:草木丛生的地方。
④ 递:遥远。
⑤ 且:将要。

清人沈德潜于《唐诗别裁集》评此诗说:"写人情物性,每在有意无意间。"可谓十分妥帖。诗人通过描写辞官归隐嵩山途中所见的景色,抒发了恬静淡泊的闲适心情。首联写归隐出发时的情景。嵩山,古称"中岳",在今河南省西部。颔联写水写鸟,其实乃托物寄情,写自己归山悠然自得之情,如流水归隐之心不改,如禽鸟至暮知还。颈联写荒城古渡、落日秋山,是寓情于景,反映诗人感情上的波折变化。尾联写山之高,点明作者的归隐地点和归隐宗旨。全诗质朴清新,自然天成,尤其是中间两联,移情于物,寄情于景,意象疏朗,感情浓郁。诗人随意写来,不见斧凿之迹,却得精巧蕴藉之妙。

Coming Back to Mount Song

A clear stream flows along a prairie green;
A cab and horse goes not in haste between.
The running water welcomes fallen bloom;
Together birds fly back in evening gloom.
An age-old ferry leads to dreary town,
The mountain dyed in sunset up and down.
Its range extends east to west, far away;
Behind closed door a hermit here would stay.

终南山

太乙①近天都,
连山到海隅②。
白云回望合,
青霭③入看无。
分野中峰变,
阴晴众壑殊④。
欲投人处宿,
隔水问樵夫。

① 太乙:即终南山。
② 海隅(yú):海边。终南山并不到海,此为夸张之词。
③ 霭(ǎi):云气。
④ 分野中峰变,阴晴众壑殊:形容终南山占地极广,使得中峰两侧的分野都变了,各个山谷的天气也阴晴不同。

首联写远景,用夸张手法勾画了终南山的总轮廓。颔联写近景,诗人走出茫茫云海,前面是蒙蒙青霭,仿佛可以触摸到,然而走进去,不但摸不着,也看不见了,可谓可望而不可即。颈联高度概括,尺幅万里。诗人站在终南山的最高峰上四面遥望,看到了终南山地域广大,占据了几个分野,山谷中沟壑纵横,以致向阳的山谷和背阴的山谷阴晴各不相同,足见终南山地域之广大。尾联"欲投人处宿,隔水问樵夫",则山之辽阔荒远可知,意蕴深厚,令人回味无穷。

Mount Eternal South

The highest peak scrapes the blue sky;
It extends from hills to the sea.
When I look back, clouds veil the eye;
When I come near, I see mist flee.
Peaks change color from left to right,
Vales differ in shade or sunbeam.
Seeking a place to pass the night,
I ask a woodman across the stream.

观　猎

风劲角弓鸣，
将军猎渭城。
草枯鹰眼疾①，
雪尽马蹄轻。
忽过新丰市，
还归细柳营②。
回看射雕处，
千里暮云平③。

① 疾：敏锐。

② 细柳营：代指打猎将军的居所。

③ 暮云平：傍晚时分云和地面连成一片的景象。

这首诗，上篇写出猎，下篇写猎归，起得突兀，结得意远，上下篇一气流走，承转自如，有格律束缚不住的气势，又能首尾回环映带，体合五律，这是章法之妙。诗中藏三地名而使人不觉，用典浑化无迹，写景俱能传情，三、四句既穷极物理又意见于言外，这是句法之妙。"枯""尽""疾""轻""忽过""还归"，遣词用字准确锤炼，咸能照应，这是字法之妙。所有这些手法，又都能巧妙表达诗中人生气远出的意态与豪情。所以，此诗完全当得起盛唐佳作的称誉。

Hunting

Louder than gusty winds twang horn-backed bows;
Hunting outside the town the general goes.
Keener o'er withered grass his falcon's eye,
Lighter on melted snow his steed trots by.
No sooner is New Harvest Market passed
Than he comes back to Willow Camp at last.
He looks back where he shot down vultures bare
Only to find cloud on cloud spread o'er there.

汉江临泛

楚塞三湘接,
荆门九派通。
江流天地外,
山色有无中。
郡邑①浮前浦②,
波澜动远空。
襄阳好风日,
留醉与山翁。

① 郡邑:城镇。
② 浦:水边。

开元二十八年(740),王维因公务去南方,此诗便是诗人途经襄阳城,欣赏汉江景色时所作,可谓是王维融画法入诗的力作。首联,以接"三湘"、通"九派"的浩渺水势一笔勾勒出汉江雄浑壮阔的景色,诗人将不可目击之景概写总述,纳浩浩江流于画边,为整个画面渲染了气氛。颔联,"天地外""有无中",为诗歌平添了一种迷茫、玄远、无可穷尽的意境。这是画家的笔意和构图层次感。颈联,"浮""动"两个动词用得极妙,使诗人笔下之景活起来,诗人泛舟江上怡然自得的心态也从中表现了出来,江水磅礴的气势亦被表现了出来。尾联诗人直抒胸臆,要与山翁共谋一醉,流露出对襄阳风物的热爱之情。

A View of the River Han

Three southern rivers rolling by,

Nine tributaries meeting here.

Their water flows from earth to sky;

Hills now appear, now disappear.

Towns seem to float on rivershore;

With waves horizons rise and fall.

Such scenery as we adore

Would make us drink and drunken all.

使①至塞上

① 使：出使。

单车②欲问边，
属国过居延。
征蓬③出汉塞，
归雁入胡天④。
大漠⑤孤烟直，
长河⑥落日圆。
萧关⑦逢候骑⑧，
都护在燕然。

② 单车：一辆车。

③ 征蓬：随风飞向远处的枯蓬。

④ 胡天：胡人的领地，此处指被唐军占领的北方。

⑤ 大漠：大沙漠，此处指凉州以北的沙漠。

⑥ 长河：有争议，经考证应指流经凉州以北沙漠的一条河，即今石羊河。

⑦ 萧关：古关名，又名陇山关。

⑧ 候骑：负责侦察和传递信息的骑兵。

《使至塞上》是王维边塞诗的代表作。诗人描写了出使塞上旅程中所见的塞外风光、生活及心情。本诗的"大漠孤烟直，长河落日圆"一联是脍炙人口的名句。边疆沙漠浩瀚无边，少有奇观异景，烽火台燃起的那一股浓烟就显得格外醒目，因此称作"孤烟"。一个"孤"字写出了景物的单调，紧接一个"直"字，却又表现了它的劲拔、坚毅之美。沙漠

On Mission to the Frontier

A single carriage goes to the frontier;

An envoy crosses northwest mountains high.

Like tumbleweed I leave the fortress drear;

As wild geese I come 'neath Tartarian sky.

In boundless desert lonely smoke rises straight;

Over endless river the sun sinks round.

I meet a cavalier at the camp gate;

In northern fort the general will be found.

上没有山峦林木,那横贯其间的黄河,就非用一个"长"字不能表达诗人的感觉。落日,本来容易给人以感伤的印象,这里用一"圆"字,却给人以亲切温暖而又苍茫的感觉。一个"圆"字,一个"直"字,用得可谓是"十二分力量",不仅准确地描绘了沙漠的景象,而且表现了作者的深切感受。诗人把孤寂的情绪巧妙地融化在广阔的自然景象的描绘中。

秋夜独坐

独坐悲双鬓,
空堂欲①二更②。
雨中山果落,
灯下草虫鸣。
白发终难变,
黄金不可成。
欲知除老病③,
唯有学无生④。

① 欲:接近。
② 二更:晚上九时至十一时。
③ 老病:衰老和生病。
④ 无生:佛家语,认为世本虚幻,万物实体无生无灭。

王维中年奉佛,诗多禅意。这首诗写出一个思想觉悟即禅悟的过程。从情入理,以情证理。诗的前半篇从人生转到草木昆虫的生存,发现这无知的草木昆虫同有知的人一样,都在无情的时光、岁月的消逝中零落哀鸣。诗人由此得到启发诱导,自以为觉悟了。诗的后半篇从诗人自己嗟老的忧伤,想到了宣扬神仙长生不老的道教。诗人感叹"黄金不可成",就是否定神仙方术之事,指明炼丹服药祈求长生的虚妄,而认为只有信奉佛教,才能从根本上消除人生的悲哀,解脱生老病死的痛苦。

Sitting Alone on an Autumn Night

Sitting alone, I grieve over my hair white,

In empty room it approaches midnight.

When it rains in the hill, I hear fruit fall;

By lamplight crickets chirp in my hall.

I cannot blacken my white hair while old,

Nor can I turn a metal into gold.

If you want to get rid of ills of old age,

You can only learn from the Buddhist sage.

李处士山居

君子盈天阶①,
小人甘自免。
方随炼金客,
林上家绝巘②。
背岭花未开,
入云树深浅。
清昼犹自眠,
山鸟时一啭。

① 天阶:登天的阶梯,此处指天子左右的官署。

② 巘(yǎn):大山上的小山。

  处士,指有道德、学问而隐居不仕者。首联,字面是说李处士山居在山之高处,实喻其为人高洁、志存高远,而在朝的小人就没有这等志向。天阶即登天的石阶,引申指天子左右的官署。"甘自免"即指甘愿自免于朝官之列。颔联是说李处士的生活态度飘逸如神仙,安家在险绝的山岩上。炼金客意指炼丹的道士。绝巘是指陡峭的山峰。颈联,李处士的山居在阳光少的一面山坡,高居入云,花开稍迟。背岭是指李处士的山居在山岭的北面。尾联,指一大清早还在睡眠的时候,山鸟就开始了鸣叫。

A Scholar's Retreat

The noble in the court may stay;
The common people can be free.
You follow Taoists on their way
To live on hilltop with high glee.
You see no flowers in full bloom
But trees high and low in the cloud.
You sleep by daylight in your room,
Heedless of the birds singing loud.

渡河到清河作

泛舟大河里,
积水穷天涯。
天波①忽开拆,
郡邑千万家。
行复见城市,
宛然②有桑麻。
回瞻旧乡国,
淼漫连云霞。

① 天波:天空的云气。

② 宛然:清晰的样子。

河,指黄河。清河,指唐贝州治所清河县,在今河北清河西。诗中描绘的是黄河下游的景致,深沉、壮观、气势磅礴。先是从水天一色开拆的缝中,看见"郡邑千万家",然后看见城市,接着是城外的农田,读之令人如见如闻。结尾两句描写作者回首时,只看见河水连天,看不见故乡了,由此抒思乡之情,发人遐思,言已尽而意未穷。

Crossing the Yellow River

I cross the River when water runs high,

Its waves surge up to the end of the sky.

Over white-crested billows rises a town,

With ten thousands of houses up and down.

Farther on stand villages amid the trees,

In the shade of hemp or of mulberries.

Looking back, but my homeland can't be seen,

I see rainbow cloud blend with foliage green.

酬虞部苏员外过蓝田别业不见留之作

贫居依谷口,
乔木带荒村。
石路枉回驾,
山家谁候门?
渔舟胶冻浦,
猎火烧寒原。
唯有白云外,
疏钟闻夜猿。

题解:虞部,工部四司之一,置员外郎一人,掌京城街巷种植、山泽苑囿及草木薪炭等事。蓝田别业即辋川别业。不见留指苏员外访王维不遇,没有在辋川停留。首联讲王维贫居在辋川谷口,高高的林木围绕着村庄。颔联讲苏员外屈尊见访却不遇而返。颈联说冬日里渔船被冻在河里,猎犬在寒冷的原野上奔跑。尾联承接颈联的描写,进一步展示了冬日荒村的薄暮凄清景象,白云外还能听到猿啼声。后四句借景表现了诗人归来后见苏员外已去的怅惘心情。

For a Visitor Impromptu to My Blue Field

My hut's at the mouth of the vale,

Wasteland belted with trees turning pale.

You care not for the rugged way

Where none waits on you all the day.

On frozen stream none fish in vain;

No hunter hunts on wintry plain.

Only beyond the freecy cloud,

Bells sparsely ring and apes wail loud.

酬比部杨员外暮宿琴台朝跻①书阁率尔②见赠之作

① 跻：登，上升。
② 率尔：无拘无束，随意。

旧简拂尘看，
鸣琴候月弹。
桃源迷汉姓，
松树有秦官。
空谷归人少，
青山背日寒。
羡君栖隐处，
遥望白云端。

　　这首诗是王维为一位弃官归隐的好友所作。首联，看简、弹琴者"拂尘""候月"，增添了许多情致。颔联两句对仗精工，叙事妥帖，景致之佳令人向往。颈联颇有意外，描述的与前面璀璨烂漫之景相反，此处则是一派清幽清冷意象，以此象征高士心志之卓越，罕有可及。一冷一热、一明一暗体现员外身处红尘又超越红尘之高远心志。

Reply to Financier Yang on His Visit to the Lute Terrace

You read the classics, dusting old bamboo;
You play music on lute as moonbeams do.
You forget your name in Peach Blossom Land;
Your pine has given shade to royal hand.
Few visit a deserted vale so old;
Mountains after sunset exhale breath cold.
Your hermitage's an admirable sight,
Viewed from afar, it is atop cloud white.

送张五归山

送君尽惆怅,
复送何人归?
几日同携手,
一朝先拂衣①。 ①拂衣：振衣而去，此处指归隐。
东山有茅屋,
幸为扫荆扉。
当亦谢官②去, ②谢官：辞官。
岂令心事违?

张五本名张諲(yīn)，兄弟排行第五。官至刑部员外郎，擅长山水画，是王维的丹青之友，两人以兄弟相称，亲如手足。张諲天宝中辞官归隐，这首诗就是作于此时，表达了诗人送别张五时引发的归隐之意。天宝中后期，杨国忠把持朝政，诗人看着一个个志同道合的朋友离开朝廷，也就产生了一种拂衣而去的心态，可是直到天宝末年，王维也没有辞官。

Seeing Zhang the Fifth Back to the Mountain

Back to the Mountain
Gloomy to part with you,
When shall I say adieu?
Together a few days,
Now you are on your way.
To your cot in hills green,
Will you keep mine as clean?
I'll leave then for the hill
And fulfil my heart's will.

喜祖三至留宿

门前洛阳客,
下马拂征衣①。　　　　　　　　　① 征衣:旅行的人穿的衣服。
不枉故人驾,
平生多掩扉。
行人返深巷,
积雪带余晖。
早岁同袍②者,　　　　　　　　　② 同袍:指朋友之间关系很好。
高车何处归?

　　祖三,即祖咏,排行第三,盛唐著名诗人。这首诗作于开元十三年(725)冬,王维在济州任上。他的老朋友祖咏及第授官后东行赴任,路过济州,王维留他在家中过夜,写了这首诗送给他。在看似平淡的诗句背后,我们读出了诗人内心的寂寞、茫然,当然也有无法掩饰的孤傲和与故旧的友情。

For Zu the Third Passing the Night with Me

From far away you come so near,
Dismount and dust yourself off here.
To show you welcome of my heart,
My oft-closed door is kept apart.
You do not think my cot obscure,
The snow you bring makes sunlight pure.
Oh, dear friend of so long ago,
Where will your car tomorrow go?

冬晚对雪忆胡居士家

寒更传晓箭①,
清镜览衰颜。
隔牖②风惊竹,
开门雪满山。
洒空深巷静,
积素广庭闲。
借问袁安舍,
翛然③尚闭关。

① 晓箭:拂晓时漏壶中指示时刻的箭。

② 牖(yǒu):窗户。

③ 翛(xiāo)然:无拘无束的样子。

胡居士是一位虔诚信佛、安贫守道的人。此诗通过对雪怀人,流露了诗人悲天悯人的慈悲情怀。首联,凛凛寒夜,更鼓报晓,诗人起来对着清冷的镜子自照,容颜憔悴。颔联,一个"惊"字最能传大雪之神,是写雪的名句,写出了大雪的浩莽气势。颈联,亦是描写深巷、庭院雪景的名句。尾联,典出《后汉书·袁安传》。袁安贫居洛阳,一次下了一丈深的大雪,一般人家都出来扫雪,只有袁安没有。洛阳令以为他已经死在家中,命人扫雪而入,却发现他安卧在床,他说:"大雪天人们都在挨饿,不宜出来乞食。"洛阳令认为他有德行,举为孝廉。

For a Buddhist Friend on a Snowing Night

The day is dawning at slow pace;
In mirror I see wrinkled face.
Outside bamboos shiver in breeze;
Doors open, snow-clad mountains freeze.
Flakes sprinkle deep in quiet lane;
In courtyard wide white piles remain.
May I ask my friend in his room
If he is musing in the gloom?

归辋川作

谷口疏钟动,
渔樵稍欲稀。
悠然远山暮,
独向白云归。
菱蔓弱难定,
杨花轻易飞。
东皋①春草色,　　　　　　　　　　① 皋(gāo)：水边高地。
惆怅掩柴扉。

诗人隐退辋川，只是半官半隐。所谓"归辋川作"，是诗人下朝归来所作。首联，傍晚时谷口的钟声缓慢地敲响了，路上行走的渔夫樵子渐渐稀少了。颔联，诗人忧愁地眺望暮色苍茫的远山，独自一人向白云生处回去。颈联，看似写景，菱颈细弱、杨花轻浮，实则写朝廷里趋炎附势的小人。尾联，东皋，唐代诗人常指自己的隐居之地。看到这一片青草，诗人惆怅地回家关上了大门。

Back to My Waterside Cottage

The evening bell tolls parting day,

Few fishermen on homeward way.

Far-off hills dissolved in twilight,

Alone I come back with cloud white.

Frail duckweeds seem to sway and swing,

Light willow down wafts on the wing.

Eastern fields dyed in vernal hue,

Gloomy, I close the door anew.

山居即事

寂寞①掩柴扉,
苍茫对落晖。
鹤巢②松树遍,
人访荜门③稀。
绿竹含新粉④,
红莲落故衣。
渡头灯火起,
处处采菱归。

① 寂寞:寂静无声。

② 巢:栖息。

③ 荜(bì)门:荆竹编成的门,常用于形容房屋简陋。

④ 新粉:指竹子刚长出来时竹节周围会带有的白色茸粉。

　　此首可以与上首《归辋川作》连读,不过这首写的是秋景。即事者当前的事物,类似以当前事物为题材的诗古人称为"即事诗"。首联,在秋天的傍晚,诗人寂寞地掩上大门,出来一看,眼前是一片茫茫的夕阳。颔联,松树上到处都有鹤筑的巢,而来访的朋友却不多见。颈联,当年的新竹,嫩嫩的竹节上还留有一圈白色粉末,红色的荷花花瓣却开始一片片脱落。尾联,渡口的渔船上亮起了灯火,采菱的姑娘们正从四面八方归来。

Rural Life

Lonely, I close my thatched gate,
And face the misty sunset late.
Cranes make their nests among pine trees;
Few visit my cot as they please.
Bamboos sprinkled with powder new,
I seem clad in red lotus hue.
With lanterns the ferry is bright,
Maids come back with chestnuts at night.

辋川闲居

一从归白社,
不复到青门。
时倚檐前树,
远看原上村。
青菰①临水映,
白鸟向山翻。
寂寞於陵子,
桔槔方灌园。

① 青菰 (gū): 俗称茭白。

开元二十四年 (736),张九龄罢相,李林甫把持朝政,社会矛盾日趋尖锐。王维此时仍在朝为官。他倾向于张九龄的开明政治,对现实十分不满,于是心生归隐之意,在辋川购置别墅,过着亦官亦隐的生活。本篇便作于这段时期,是其隐逸生活的真实写照。"青菰临水映,白鸟向山翻"一句,诗人以画家的眼光来观察自然景物,抓住眼前景物最鲜明的形象来勾画:青翠的茭白掩映在清冽的水中,白鸟展翅翻飞于苍茫的山间。色彩相互映衬,景致动静结合,自然奇妙。

Leisurely Life by Riverside

Come back to my White Hermitage,

I've not gone near the door of sage.

At times I lean on courtyard tree

To see rural scene before me.

The paddy fields turn water green;

White birds whirl against mountain screen.

The lonely hermit tries to sprinkle

His garden from the pools which wrinkle.

春园即事

宿雨乘轻屐,
春寒著弊袍。
开畦①分白水,
间柳发红桃。
草际成棋局,
林端举桔槔②。
还持鹿皮几,
日暮隐蓬蒿。

① 畦(qí):田园里分成的一块一块区域。

② 桔(jié)槔(gāo):井上汲水的工具。

诗歌流动着自然的美景和诗人安闲恬适的情怀,清新优美。红桃绿柳,桔槔(古代井上汲水的工具)起落,畦开水流,一片春意盎然的景象。在这良辰美景之中,摆棋对局,凭几蓬蒿,其乐也融融。如画般的景象,似梦般的意境,一切都是那么清幽绮丽,赏心悦目。

Spring in My Garden

I put on clogs: it rained last night;
Shabby clad, I feel cold in spring.
In my furrows flows water white,
And budding willows spread the wing.
Like chessboard looks my meadow green;
The winch rises high as a tree.
Resting my elbow on deer skin,
At sunset amid weeds I'm free.

淇上田园即事

屏居①淇水上，
东野旷无山。
日隐桑柘②外，
河明闾井③间。
牧童望村去，
猎犬随人还。
静者④亦何事？
荆扉乘昼关。

① 屏居：隐居。

② 柘 (zhè)：柘树。

③ 闾 (lǘ) 井：村落。

④ 静者：深得清静之道的人，此处为作者自指。

这首诗是王维隐居淇上时所作，描绘了淇上小村傍晚时的优美恬静的田园风光。淇上，淇水边上。淇水发源于河南，流入卫河，在今河南登封市。诗人于开元十四年（726）自济州离任到淇上为官，不久即在淇上弃官隐居。屏居即指隐居。静者是指深得清静之道、超然恬静的人，此处是作者自指。

My Garden by Riverside

Living with ease by riverside,

I see no hills in east plain wide.

The sun sinks beyond mulberries;

The stream flows between cots and trees.

The shepherds to the village go;

Hunters come back with hound and bow.

What shall I do, looking before?

Though it is noon, I'll close my door.

晚春[1]与严少尹与诸公见过

[1] 晚春:春季第三个月。

松菊荒三径,
图书共五车。
烹葵[2]邀上宾,
看竹到贫家。
鹊乳[3]先春草,
莺啼过落花。
自怜黄发暮,
一倍惜年华。

[2] 葵:葵菜,嫩叶可食用。

[3] 乳:动词,喜鹊养育幼鸟。

这首诗作于乾元元年(758)春末。严少尹,即严武。诗人隐居的地方虽然荒凉,但是长满了松树和菊花,同时家里还有很多的藏书。所谓的葵,即我国古代一种重要的蔬菜,有苋葵、凫葵、楚葵等,其嫩叶皆可食。显然这样的食物不是豪门所用,而为隐士所食。诗人烹制葵菜邀请尊贵的宾客,来到贫穷简陋的家里欣赏青竹。所谓的乳,《说文》解释为"人及鸟生子曰乳"。这时候春草刚刚生长,鸟雀已经开始哺乳,鸟雀啼叫着飞过春天刚刚开败的落花。黄发指长寿老人。看着春天的美景,诗人自怜自叹自己年纪很老了,一定要加倍珍惜年华,享受这美好闲适的时光。

For Vice-Prefect Yan and Others in Late Spring

My lane'd be waste without chrysanthemum and pine,
I have five carloads of script nothing can outdo.
For my distinguished friends I've prepared greens and wine,
You won't neglect my humble cot for its bamboo.
My magpies brood their young before spring breeds green grass;
My orioles sing on fallen flowers and shed tears.
How can I not regret my hair turns grey, alas!
Can I make double use of my remaining years?

过①感化寺昙兴上人山院

① 过：过访。

暮持筇竹②杖，
相待虎溪头。
催客闻山响，
归房逐水流。
野花丛发好，
谷鸟一声幽。
夜坐空林寂，
松风直似秋。

② 筇(qióng)竹：一种竹子，适宜作拐杖。

这首诗是王维游览寺观的诗作。上人是对长老和尚的尊称。首联引"虎溪"为句，叙述了上人手持竹杖在寺外等候诗人。筇，古书上说的一种竹子，可以做手杖。虎溪，是千年古村，位于蓝田县境西北与宁远县交界之地，因村后石山如虎形，村前溪水潺流不绝，故以"虎溪"为名。颔联是说山中的泉水声仿佛在催促客人进门，诗人和上人一起顺着水流回到了山院。山响即山泉流水声。颈联描写了回到山院所见到的景致。尾联描写了诗人在山寺夜坐的景象。

For Buddhist Tanxing in His Temple

You come at dusk, a bamboo cane in hand,
To wait for me at the creek of Tiger's land.
The mountain seems to roar to hasten me
To go to your temple with the stream free.
How much we like wild flowers in full bloom!
The song of a bird breaks the valley's gloom.
At night you muse in empty forest still,
The breeze brings through the pines an autumn chill.

郑果州相过

丽日照残春,
初晴草木新。
床前磨镜客,
林里灌园人。
五马①惊穷巷,
双童②逐老身。
中厨办粗饭,
当恕阮家贫。

① 五马:太守的车。
② 双童:指代仆人。

这首诗以鲜明的色彩对比,用"丽日""残春""草木"等意象勾勒出一幅清新自然的暮春画卷,为郑果州的来访做环境烘托。接着以"磨镜客""灌园人"自比隐士。诗人用一个"惊"字写出了巷子的幽深与清寂,与贾岛的"僧敲月下门"的"敲"有异曲同工之妙。诗的最后,以阮家贫来自谦,委婉地表达唯恐招待不周之意。整首诗隐隐地透出诗人不慕富贵的傲骨,宁静淡泊的心境以及旷达幽远的胸襟,暗含王维出仕超脱的禅心。

On Governor Zheng's Visit

The sun has beautified the waning spring;
After the shower grass looks fresh and green.
A hermit cannot do a better thing
Than water his garden and make it clean.
Your horse and carriage have woken the lane;
We come to welcome you, father and son.
But I have only coarse food to entertain.
Excuse me if it is not better done.

送钱少府还蓝田

草色日向好,
桃源人去稀。
手持平子赋,
目送老莱衣。
每候山樱发,
时同海燕归。
今年寒食酒,
应是返柴扉。

这首送别诗的送别地点是长安。钱少府即钱起,时任蓝田县尉。首联里提到的桃源系指蓝田辋川。颔联的平子赋系指张衡的《归田赋》,意指"仕不得志,欲归于田"。老莱子特别孝敬父母,年七十而父母犹在,经常身着五彩斑斓的花衣,学小孩儿的样子,哄逗其父母开心。颈联是说钱起总是在樱花开时就准时到辋川探视父母,好像燕子一样,每到春天时就会准时到来。尾联是说今年寒食节的时候,诗人也会回蓝田。

Seeing Qian Qi Off to His Blue Field

Grass grows more lush from day to day,
To Peach Bloom Land few on the way.
With your Home-going Song in hand,
I see you off to your homeland.
Go when cherries blossom with glee
And swallows come back from the sea.
You'll drink on Cold Food Day this year
When at your door you will appear.

送杨长史赴果州

褒斜不容幰①,
之子去何之?
鸟道②一千里,
猿啼十二时。
官桥祭酒③客,
山木女郎祠。
别后同明月,
君应听子规。

① 幰 (xiǎn): 车幔,此处代指车辆。

② 鸟道: 狭窄的山路。

③ 祭酒: 饯别酒。

首联讲褒斜栈道悠长而狭窄,不知道杨长史通过这条古栈道去哪里。褒斜,古栈道,在秦岭山脉中贯穿关中平原与汉中盆地的山谷。南口曰褒,北口曰斜,长凡235公里。不容幰,是指道路狭窄。颔联继续描写道路的狭长和野外跋涉的艰难,只有小鸟可以飞过。颈联中的官桥是指官道上的桥梁。祭酒客则是指祖道登程的旅客。此联仍指蜀道的艰难,行必有祈祷。尾联,离别后联系诗人和杨长史的唯一纽带就是那同一轮明月,而子规之啼叫会更加让旅人有思归之情。

Seeing Prefect Yang Off to Guozhou

It's difficult to pass the dale.

Why should you go so far away?

There are long miles for birds to sail

And for apes to wail night and day.

For safety you should pray with wine;

To see sights you'd pass hills and streams.

After we part, the moon's still fine.

Forget not cuckoo's song in dreams!

送邢桂州

铙[①]吹喧京口,
风波下洞庭。
赭圻将赤岸,
击汰[②]复扬舲。
日落江湖白,
潮来天地青。
明珠归合浦,
应逐使臣星。

① 铙(náo)吹:军中乐歌。

② 击汰:用桨击水划船。

　　首联,铙吹即铙歌,本是军乐,后也在庆祝活动中使用。此两句的意思是送行的鼓乐在京口热闹异常,朋友的船只将在风波中直指湖南洞庭。颔联,船夫奋力划桨,击起水波无数,船飞一般地经过了赭圻、赤岸。颈联是王维描写江南风光的名句。"白""青"二字最为传神,沈德潜称赞其为"奇警"。尾联用典见《后汉书·孟尝传》中"合浦还珠"的故事。诗人希望邢桂州在桂林任上,能像孟尝君那样,百废俱兴,开创"合浦还珠"的新迹象。

Seeing Commissioner Xing Off

Music is loud by riverside,

On the waves of the Lake you ride.

Banners and flags redden the shore,

With drumbeats boatmen dip their oar.

From sunset water takes its dye;

The tide turns earth as blue as sky.

When pearls are returned from afar,

The envoy comes down like a star.

凉州郊外游望

野老①才三户②,
边村少四邻。
婆娑依里社,
箫鼓赛田神。
洒酒浇刍狗,
焚香拜木人。
女巫纷屡舞,
罗袜自生尘。

① 野老:村野的老人。
② 三户:此处指人很少。

凉州是唐代西部军事重镇,位于今甘肃省武威市,是古代丝绸之路河西走廊段的门户。这首诗描写唐代凉州地区赛神的民俗,颇具乡土气息。甘肃一带少数民族能歌善舞,这也是我国西部少数民族的共同特点。"赛田神"固然是一种带有迷信色彩的活动,但却是当时边地百姓"知恩图报"纯朴品性的体现。

A Rustic Scene on the Border

A village has three cots or four,

On the frontier neighbors are few.

The shrine sees people dance before

And hears drumbeats and flute songs anew.

On dogs of straw wine is poured out,

Incense burned for idols of wood.

Witches in shoes dance all about,

Their stockings dusted to no good.

春日上方即事

好读高僧传,
时看辟谷①方。
鸠形将刻杖,
龟壳用支床。
柳色青山映②,
梨花夕鸟藏。
北窗桃李下,
闲坐但焚香。

① 辟谷:道教的一种修炼术,辟谷时,除药物外不食。

② 映:同"掩",遮掩的意思。

上方即山上之佛寺。本诗描写了诗人在日常生活中的学禅经历,体现出了诗人对佛学的喜爱以及深厚的佛学造诣。首联描写了寺中僧人的爱好。高僧传,泛指高僧之传记。辟谷是一种修炼方法,屏除谷食。颔联指寺僧非常老了,生活中有很多古朴之趣。颈联点出了山寺环境怡人适于修炼,柳色、青山、梨花、夕鸟相映成趣。尾联是指在如此幽雅的环境里老僧还可以闲坐焚香静修。

For a Buddhist in His Cell

The Buddhist History's what you read;
A meagre meal is what you need.
A turtledove carved on your cane,
Tortoise shells 'neath your bed remain.
Mountains are green with willow trees;
Birds nest amid peach blooms with ease.
By the window beside peach flowers
You burn incense in leisure hours.

登裴迪秀才小台

端居不出户,
满目望云山。
落日鸟边下,
秋原人外闲。
遥知远林际,
不见此檐间。
好客多乘月,
应门莫上关①。

① 关:门闩。

起句,王夫之评曰"拙好"。所谓的拙,即是纯朴而看似平淡无奇,所谓的好则是精工而伤神。两者自然的融合实为难得。"落日鸟边下,秋原人外闲"句法倒转,尽展晚景之妙,可谓诗境最精彩处。

On the Garden Terrace of Pei Di

Staying at home, you needn't go out,
But see clouds and hills all about.
When birds alight with setting sun,
On autumn plain busy is none.
My cot's in the woods far away,
I can't see the roof where you stay.
So I visit you by moonlight
And leave my door unclosed at night.

千塔主人

逆旅逢佳节,
征帆未可前。
窗临汴河水,
门渡楚人船。
鸡犬散墟①落,　　　　　　　　① 墟(xū)落:村落。
桑榆荫远田。
所居人不见,
枕席生云烟。

这首诗颇具首尾浑融之趣。诗仍是客愁他乡的旧调,但是在首联点明客情之后,即搁笔转调,远眺之处是一派闲云淡墨。这与诗人心胸的开拓、视域的延展是密不可分的。颔联的"窗临""门渡"两句,尺幅千里之势,正见其心胸。颈联"鸡犬""桑榆"两句,颇具五柳先生乐居田园之风范。尾联回环诗题,为点睛之妙笔。"人不见"已堪称幻境,而妙思枕席云烟之升腾,可臻于化境矣。

For a Hermit Under the Pagoda

I at an inn must pass the holiday,

My boat cannot go on its forward way.

Your window looks on northern rivershore;

East-going ships pass by your southern door.

Here and there dogs and chickens can be seen;

The plain is shaded by mulberries green.

But who can see the hermit living there,

Over whose bed cloud rises in the air?

少 年 行

（四首其一）

新丰①美酒斗十千，　　　　　　　　① 新丰：县名，古时新丰县产名酒。
咸阳游侠多少年。
相逢意气为君饮，
系马高楼垂柳边。

这首诗写长安城里游侠少年意气风发的风貌和豪迈气概。"新丰美酒"与"咸阳游侠"用对举方式来写，少年游侠堪称人中之杰，新丰美酒堪称酒中之冠。新丰美酒，似乎天生就为少年游侠增色而设；少年游侠，没有新丰美酒也显不出他们的豪纵风流。第三句"相逢意气为君饮"把二者联结在一起。"意气"包含的内容很丰富，轻生报国的壮烈情怀、重义疏财的侠义性格、豪纵不羁的气质、使酒任性的作风等，都可以包含在"意气"之中。"系马高楼垂柳边"是由马、高楼、垂柳组成的一幅画面。马是侠客不可分的伴侣。高楼则正是在繁华街市上那所备有新丰美酒的华美酒楼了。高楼旁的垂柳，则与之相映成趣。它点缀了酒楼风光，使之在华美、热闹中显出雅致、飘逸，不流于市井的鄙俗。

Song of Youngsters

(I)

Young heroes cannot go without good wine,
Without them could the capital be fine?
When they meet, they will drink wine as they please,
Their horses tethered to the willow trees.

九月九日忆山东兄弟

独在异乡为异客，
每逢佳节倍思亲。
遥知兄弟登高处，
遍插茱萸①少一人。

① 茱(zhū)萸(yú)：古时人们会在重阳节插戴茱萸。

许渊冲译王维诗选

    这首诗是王维17岁时的七绝，和他后来那些富于画意、构图设色非常讲究的山水诗不同，这首抒情小诗写得非常朴素。但千百年来，人们在作客他乡的情况下读这首诗，却都强烈地感受到了它的艺术力量。诗歌的第一句用了一个"独"字，两个"异"字，分量下得很足。对亲人的思念，对自己孤孑处境的感受，都凝聚在这个"独"字里面。"异乡为异客"中的两个"异"字所造成的艺术效果，远比一般地叙说他乡作客要强烈得多。作客他乡者的思乡怀亲之情一旦遇到"佳节"——往往是家人团聚的日子——就更容易爆发出来，所以"每逢佳节倍思亲"就是十分自然的事。诗歌的后两句构思更为巧妙奇绝，诗人不说自己思乡，而是想象家乡兄弟对自己的思念。这种写离情从对方落笔的笔法在中晚唐才日渐增多。

Thinking of My Brothers on Mountain-Climbing Day

Alone, a lonely stranger in a foreign land,
I doubly pine for my kinsfolk on holiday.
I know my brothers would, with dog-weed spray in hand,
Climb up the mountain and miss me so far away.

送元二使安西

渭城朝雨浥[①]轻尘，
客舍青青柳色新。
劝君更尽一杯酒，
西出阳关无故人。

① 浥(yì)：湿。

许渊冲译王维诗选

　　本诗是一首极负盛名、千古传诵、脍炙人口的送别诗，曾被谱入乐曲，称为"渭城曲""阳关曲"或"阳关三叠"。安西是唐中央政府为统辖西域而设的都护府的简称。前两句分别写明送别时间是清晨，地点是渭城客舍，氛围是自东向西延伸不见尽头的驿道以及驿道两旁的柳树。这一切似乎都是极平常的景物，而读来却风光如画，抒情浓郁，构成了一幅色调清新明朗的图景，为这场送别提供了典型的自然环境。后两句是一个整体。朋友"西出阳关"免不了经历万里长途跋涉的艰辛与寂寞。因此，这临行之际"劝君更尽一杯酒"就更是浸透了诗人全部情义的琼浆玉液。这里不只有依依惜别的情谊与对远行者的体贴，还包含着对国家和平安宁的美好祝愿。

A Farewell Song

No dust is raised on the road wet with morning rain,
The willows by the hotel look so fresh and green.
I invite you to drink a cup of wine again,
West of the Sunny Pass no friends will be seen.

送沈子福之江东

杨柳渡头行客稀,
罟①师荡桨向临圻。
惟有相思②似春色,
江南江北送君归。

① 罟(gǔ)师:船夫。

② 相思:此处指好友之间的思念。

许渊冲译王维诗选

送别诗是王维诗歌创作中的一个重要题材,几乎首首都有新意。本诗第一句的"行客稀"三字写渡口的冷落,而其中却隐隐透出诗人此时的心情。第二句写送行者站在岸头,目送友人,心逐江波,情思悠远。这时,依依惜别变为对朋友一路行程的关心。这两句点明了环境,烘托了气氛,为下面感情的抒发做了铺垫。七绝的第三句往往最能彰显诗歌创作的功力。格调的高下、笔法的工拙,都在这一句。而本诗的第三句以春色比友情,可以说是翻空出奇,化无形为有形。人们对春色的所有美好感觉和印象,乃至古往今来骚人墨客对春色的歌咏,都成了"相思"一语的丰富内涵。

Seeing a Friend Off to the East

At willow-shaded ferry passengers are few;
Into the eastward stream the boatman puts his oars.
Only my longing heart looks like the vernal hue,
It would go with you along northern and southern shores.

伊州歌

清风明月苦①相思,
荡子②从戎十载余。
征人去日殷勤嘱,
归雁来时数附书③。

① 苦:形容到了极点。
② 荡子:此处指丈夫。
③ 附书:寄书信。

"伊州"为曲调名。王维的这首绝句是当时梨园传唱的名歌。诗的前两句,展现出一位女子在秋夜里苦苦思念远征丈夫的情景。诗的后两句运用逆挽(叙事体裁中的"倒叙")手法,引导读者随女主人公的回忆,重睹发生在10年前动人的一幕生活场景:送行女子对即将入伍的丈夫说不出更多的话,千言万语化成一句叮咛:"当大雁南归时,你可要多多地寄家书给我啊!"然而这种叮咛真的可以让在战场上出生入死、身不由己的丈夫多寄几封家书吗? 此诗艺术构思的巧妙,主要表现在"逆挽"的妙用。然而,读者只觉其平易亲切,毫不着意,娓娓动人,这正是诗艺臻于化境、炉火纯青的体现。

Song of Lovesickness

How much I long for you, seeing the moon in breeze!
You've gone to the frontier for more than ten long years.
Do you remember what I said to the wild geese:
"Bring me a letter for which I have shed vain tears!"

戏题盘石

可怜^①盘石临泉水，
复有垂杨拂酒杯。
若道春风不解意，
何因^②吹送落花来？

① 可怜：可爱。

② 何因：也作"因何"。

  这首诗写柳拂花飞的春天，诗人与朋友饮酒于大石之上的情景。全诗情绪欢畅，意境耐人寻味，充满了生机与野趣。前两句是说，真可爱啊，清泉边上卧着一块盘石，而我就坐在这盘石上饮酒，清风吹动垂杨的枝条，轻轻地抚摸着酒杯。后两句是说，如果说春风不理解人的心意，那它为什么又吹撒落花来助酒兴呢？

Written at Random on a Rock

By the fountainside stands a rock at ease;
My wine-cup is caressed by a willow tree.
Who says the vernal breeze does not know how to please?
Why does it blow down flowers up to me?

与卢员外象过崔处士兴宗林亭

绿树重阴盖四邻,

青苔日厚自无尘。

科头①箕踞②长松下,

白眼③看他世上人。

① 科头:不戴帽子,把头发挽成发髻。

② 箕(jī)踞(jù):伸展两脚而坐,表示不拘束的坐姿。

③ 白眼:此处指代蔑视。

卢员外象,即员外郎卢象,盛唐颇有名气的诗人。崔兴宗,王维的内弟,此时尚未出仕,故称处士。前两句是说,崔兴宗的林亭有一棵好大的树,枝繁叶茂,重重覆盖着四周。而树荫下青青的苔藓一天比一天厚实,自然不见有任何尘土。后两句是说,崔兴宗坐在这棵大松树下,帽子也不戴,两腿向前伸开坐着,傲慢地翻着白眼,鄙视人世间的世俗小人。全诗描画出崔兴宗强烈的爱憎分明、不拘俗礼、为人正直坦荡的精神风貌。

Cui's Bower in the Forest

Green trees cast shade on shade around;
There is no dust on mossy ground.
Sitting bare-headed 'neath pine-trees,
He looks down on those who displease.

寒食汜上作

广武城边逢暮春,
汶阳归客①泪沾巾。
落花寂寂②啼山鸟,
杨柳青青渡水③人。

① 汶阳归客：诗人自指。

② 寂寂：形容寂静无声。

③ 水：指汜水。

此诗是开元十四年（726）作者自济州西归，寒食节时经广武、汜水而作。寒食，节令名，在清明节的前一天。相传是晋文公为悼念宁被烧死而不出山的介子推所设，这一天禁止生火煮食，只吃冷食。前两句是说，诗人自济州汶阳西归，途经河南广武城，适逢暮春时节，心情悲伤。面对暮春的衰败景色，诗人胸中既有对逝去光阴的伤感，又有对未来的迷茫。后两句是说，空山中的鸟啼反而显出落花的寂寥，更衬出诗人的孤单，只有青青的杨柳仿佛与渡水的诗人依依惜别。

Cold Food Day on River Si

Spring fades when I pass by the city wall,

How can my homesick tears not fall?

Over fallen flowers mountain birds cry;

Green willows will not say to me "Goodbye!"

秋夜曲

桂魄①初生秋露微,
轻罗②已薄未更衣。
银筝③夜久殷勤弄④,
心怯空房不忍归。

① 桂魄:此处指月亮。
② 轻罗:轻薄的丝织品,此处代指夏装。
③ 筝:一种拨弦乐器。
④ 殷勤弄:频频弹拨。

此题属乐府《杂曲歌辞》,是一首婉转含蓄的闺怨诗,写初秋月夜少妇的怨情。起句写秋月从东方升起,露水虽生,却是淡薄微少,给人一种清凉之感,烘托出女主人公清冷孤寂的心情。第二句写女主人公在气候转凉的季节还穿着轻软细薄的罗衣,没有更换秋衣;暗示了因秋凉需要更衣而思念远方的丈夫。第三句写女主人公的弹筝行动,实际是以乐曲寄情。结句以巧妙的构思和奇特的表现方法,通过女主人公的心理活动,展示了她独守空房的哀怨。

Song of an Autumn Night

Chilled by light autumn dew beneath the crescent moon,
She has not changed her dress though her silk robe is thin,
Playing all night on silver lute an endless tune,
Afraid of empty room, she can't bear to go in.

奉和圣制从蓬莱向兴庆阁道中留春雨中春望之作应制[1]

[1] 应制：指应皇帝之命而作。

渭水自萦秦塞曲，
黄山旧绕汉宫斜。
銮舆[2]迥出[3]千门柳，
阁道回看上苑[4]花。
云里帝城双凤阙，
雨中春树万人家。
为乘阳气[5]行时令，
不是宸[6]游重物华[7]。

[2] 銮(luán)舆(yú)：皇帝的坐乘。

[3] 迥(jiǒng)出：远出。

[4] 上苑：此处指皇家园林。

[5] 阳气：春天的气息。

[6] 宸(chén)：指代皇帝居处，后又引伸为皇帝的代称。

[7] 华：形容美好。

蓬莱宫，即唐大明宫。唐代宫城位于长安东北，而大明宫又位于宫城东北。兴庆宫在宫城东南角。公元735年，从大明宫经兴庆宫，一直到城东南的风景区曲江，筑阁道相通。帝王后妃，可由阁道直达曲江。王维的这首七律，就是唐玄宗由阁道出游时在雨中春望赋诗的一首和作。所谓"应制"，指应皇帝之命而作。古代应制诗，大多是歌功颂德

Written in the Same Rhymes as His Majesty's Verse on a Spring Scene in Rain Written on His Way from the Fairy Palace to the Celebration Hall

The winding River passes the capital by;
The Yellow Mountains surround royal palaces high.
Magnificent carriages caressed by willow trees;
The broad way adorned with fragrant flowers to please.
Two towers pierce the cloud to scrape the azure sky,
The vernal trees shed crystalline tears far and nigh.
The royal trip is made to welcome early spring,
So even flowers in rain are gladdened to sing.

之词。王维这首诗也不例外,但诗歌的艺术性很高,王维善于抓住眼前的实际景物进行渲染。比如用春天作为背景,让帝城自然地染上一层春色;用雨中云雾缭绕来表现氤氲祥瑞的气氛,这些都显得真切而自然。这是因为王维兼有诗人和画家之长,在选取、再现帝城长安景物的时候,构图上既显得阔大美好,又足以传达处于兴盛时期帝都长安的风貌。

和贾舍人早朝

绛帻鸡人报晓筹，
尚衣①方进翠云裘。　　　　　　　　①尚衣：掌管皇家衣著的官员。
九天阊阖开宫殿，
万国衣冠拜冕旒②。　　　　　　　　②冕旒：指皇帝。
日色才临仙掌动，
香烟欲傍衮龙浮。
朝罢须裁五色诏，
佩声归到凤池③头。　　　　　　　　③凤池：指中书省。

贾至写过一首《早朝大明宫》，当时颇为人注目，杜甫、岑参亦曾作诗相和。王维的这首和作，利用细节描写和场景渲染，写出了大明宫早朝时庄严华贵的气氛，别具艺术特色。首联"报晓"和"进翠云裘"两个细节，显示了宫廷中庄严、肃穆的特点，给早朝制造气氛。颔联在"万国衣冠"之后着一"拜"字，利用数量上众与寡、位置上卑与尊的

Reply to Jia Zhi's Morning Levee

The watchmen in red hood announce the dawning day;
The attendants come with green-cloud fur on the way.
The imperial palace opens its door on door;
Envoys from foreign lands bow to the throne we adore.
You stand beside the fan-holder at first daylight,
And see the incense-sweetened dragon on the height.
Withdrawn, you write on royal paper colorful;
With pendants clinking you return to Phoenix Pool.

对比，突出了大唐帝国的威仪。"宫殿"即贾至题中的大明宫。"冕旒"本是皇帝戴的帽子，此代指皇帝。颈联通过仙掌挡日、香烟缭绕制造了一种皇廷特有的雍容华贵氛围。"仙掌"是形状如扇的仪仗，用以挡风遮日。尾联是说"朝罢"之后，皇帝有事诏告，所以贾至要到中书省凤池去用五色纸起草诏书了。

出 塞 作

居延城外猎天骄①,
白草连天野火烧。
暮云空碛②时驱马,
秋日平原好射雕③。
护羌校尉朝乘障④,
破虏将军⑤夜渡辽。
玉靶⑥角弓珠勒马⑦,
汉家将赐霍嫖姚。

① 天骄：即"天之骄子",汉代时匈奴恃强,自称"天之骄子"。此处借称唐朝的吐蕃。

② 碛（qi）：沙漠。

③ 射雕：泛指用箭射空中的鸟类。

④ 乘障：登城。

⑤ 破虏将军：此处代指唐朝守边的将领。

⑥ 玉靶：镶玉的剑柄。此处代指宝剑。

⑦ 珠勒马：马络头上用珠宝做装饰,代指骏马。

　　这首诗以出征将士的奋勇豪情与边塞战场的旷阔肃杀氛围为直接描写对象,展现了边塞题材中最激动人心的场景与最激昂奋发的精神内容。诗的前四句写敌军的气焰,后四句写汉军的胜利。诗意完全分成两半来写,这就带有歌行铺叙转换之风。全诗读来,音调铿锵,声调响亮。其中三、四句写吐蕃狩猎的场景,常为人称道。暮云低垂、空旷无边的沙漠,秋高气爽、牧草枯黄的平原,以开阔的气势勾勒出敌兵的强悍勇猛。

Out of the Frontier

The proud Tartar sons are hunting out of the town,
White grass spreads to the sky, wild fire burns up and down.
They ride on the desert when evening clouds hang low;
In autumn days on the vast plain they bend their bow.
Our officers strengthen their defense by daylight;
Our victorious generals cross the river at night.
The swords, bows and bridles mounted with gems and jade
Are awarded generals and their brave cavalcade.

春日与裴迪过新昌里访吕逸人不遇

桃源一向^①绝风尘,
柳市南头访隐沦^②。
到门不敢题凡鸟^③,
看竹何须问主人?
城外青山如屋里,
东家流水入西邻。
闭户著书多岁月,
种松皆老作龙鳞。

① 一向:从过去到现在的一段时间。

② 隐沦:隐居的人。

③ 题凡鸟:典出《世说新语·简傲》。魏嵇康与吕安两人平素非常要好,只要一想念对方,便专程前去探望。有一次,吕安拜访嵇康时,嵇康不在家,嵇康的哥哥嵇喜前来迎接。吕安不进屋,只在门上写了一个"凤"字就走了,"凤"的繁体字字形可被拆为"凡"与"鸟"这两个字,这是吕安在讥讽嵇喜,认为他只不过是一只"凡鸟"而已。此处作者在"题凡鸟"前加"不敢",一是为了说明此次来访未碰到主人,二是赞扬吕逸不俗气。

王维和裴迪是知交,早年一同住在终南山,常相唱和,以后,两人又在辋川山庄"浮舟往来,弹琴赋诗,啸咏终日"。新昌里在长安城内。吕逸人即吕姓隐士,事迹未详。这首诗极赞吕逸人闭户著书的隐居生活,句句流露出对吕逸人的钦羡之情,以至青山、流水、松树,都为诗人所爱慕,充分表现了诗人归隐皈依的情思。描写中虚实结合,有上下句虚实相间的,也有上下联虚实相对的,笔姿灵活,变化多端,既不空泛,又不呆滞,颇有情味。

Visit to an Absent Hermit

Like the Peach Blossom Land far from Vanity Fair,
South of Willow Market we visit the hermit there.
We arrive at his door to find the phoenix out,
If you like the bamboo, what should you ask about?
Mountains are green viewed from without as from within;
From east to west water will run out and flow in.
Behind the door he's been writing from year to year,
Like dragon's scale the bark of pine planted here.

积雨辋川庄作

积雨空林烟火迟,
蒸藜①炊黍②饷③东菑④。
漠漠水田飞白鹭,
阴阴夏木啭黄鹂。
山中习静观朝槿⑤,
松下清斋折露葵。
野老与人争席罢,
海鸥何事更相疑?

① 藜(lí):一年生草本植物,嫩叶可食。

② 黍(shǔ):一种谷物,古时为主食。

③ 饷:送饭食到田头。

④ 菑(zī):已经开垦了一年的田地。

⑤ 槿(jǐn):植物名。花朝开夕谢,因此常被引用以感叹人生枯荣无常。

此诗以清新的笔触,描写了久雨之后的辋川风光。全诗将辋川庄恬淡静谧的田园景致与自己闲适安逸的禅寂生活结合起来,创造出一派人与自然和谐相处、陶然忘机的空灵境界。特别是颔联两句,写景精致,天然入妙,历来为人所称道。"漠漠""阴阴"两组叠字,不但增加了诗的音韵,而且开拓了诗的境界。有了"漠漠",水田就显得广阔辽远,白鹭便有了自由飞翔的空间;有了"阴阴",才显得雨后树林的荫浓幽深,烘托出黄鹂鸣唱的婉转清丽。同时,白鹭之"白",黄鹂之"黄",作为两点亮色映衬于空濛的背景中,更显得鲜明。

Rainy Days in My Riverside Hermitage

After long rain cooking fire's made late in the village;
Millet and greens are cooked for those doing tillage.
Over the boundless paddy fields egrets fly;
In gloomy summer forest golden orioles cry.
In quiet hills I watch short-lived blooms as I please,
And eat sunflower seeds under the green pine trees.
With other villagers I would not disagree;
Even sea gulls from far away would come near me.

寒食城东即事

清溪一道穿桃李,
演漾①绿蒲涵白芷。
溪上人家凡②几家,
落花半落东流水。
蹴鞠③屡过飞鸟上,
秋千竞出垂杨里。
少年分日④作遨游,
不用清明兼上巳。

① 演漾:荡漾。
② 凡:总共。
③ 蹴(cù)鞠(jū):古时候踢球的游戏。
④ 分日:安排好日期。

    此诗大概是王维少年时漫游两京期间的作品。这首诗勾画出一幅唐代寒食节游春的风俗画。画面上都是年轻人,男的踢球,女的荡秋千,玩得很高兴。而桃花、李花、清溪、流水、人家、飞鸟、垂杨,都是年轻人的陪衬。整首诗传递出一派生气盎然、雀跃兴奋的景象。

Cold Food Day in the East of the Town

A limpid stream threads through peach and plum trees,
Green duckweeds and water plants sway with ease.
How many people live by riverside?
Half of the flowers fall with ebbing tide.
As flying birds a ball is kicked high;
Green willows send the swing to kiss the sky.
The youngsters want to make excursions gay;
They need not wait until the vernal day.

早秋山中作

无才不敢累明时①,
思向东溪守故篱。
岂厌尚平婚嫁早,
却嫌陶令去官迟。
草间蛩响临秋急,
山里蝉声薄暮悲。
寂寞柴门人不到,
空林独与白云期。

① 明时:指政治清明的时代。

这首诗当作于开元末年,首联写自己没有杰出的才能,不敢连累了圣明的朝代,想着要弃官回嵩山东溪隐居。当然"无才"是作者的愤激反语,流露了怀才不遇的情绪。颔联直抒胸臆:我不厌弃尚平早早办完了儿女婚嫁之事就出游山川的行为,相反,我还觉得陶渊明弃官归隐有点太迟。颈联景中寓情,一语双关。蟋蟀急叫,知了悲鸣,既写山中环境的孤寂、凄清,又暗示诗人内心的孤独、悲凉。尾联承上联而来,写柴门寂寞,人烟稀少,环境如此凄清,所以作者只好与山林为伍,与白云做伴了。

Written in the Mountain in Early Autumn

A talentless man may spoil a spring day,
To my cot by East Stream I'd go my way.
From others' marriage I'd like to be free,
And I've resigned my office with high glee.
I'd welcome autumn with its crickets' song,
But grieve not with cicadas all day long.
Not lonely with no visitor in sight,
In empty woods I'd be friend with cloud white.

陇 西 行

十里一走①马,
五里一扬鞭。
都护军书至,
匈奴围酒泉。
关山正飞雪,
烽戍②断无烟。

① 走:跑,奔驰。

② 烽戍:古代用烽火和狼烟报警的土堡哨所。

此诗作于出使凉州期间。《陇西行》是乐府古题之一,属相和歌辞瑟调曲。首两句运用夸张手法,写递送军书,驿马疾驰的情状:马鞭一扬就跑了五里,一阵狂奔就是十里。然后再补叙原因,实实在在。谋篇布局,井然有序。为什么快马传书?原因是吐蕃包围了酒泉。由于漫天飞雪,边境的烽火台无法燃烟报警,只有以快马驰报敌兵来犯的消息。

Song of the Frontier

A horse is galloping;
A man flips up and down.
What message does he bring?
The siege of border town.
It's snowing on the height,
No beacon fire in sight.

送　别

下马饮①君酒，
问君何所之？
君言不得意，
归卧②南山陲③。
但去莫复问，
白云无尽时。

① 饮：使……喝。

② 归卧：隐居。

③ 陲：边缘。

　　这是首送别友人归隐的诗歌，诗歌采用问答的方式从友人口中说出归隐的原因，表现出诗人复杂的思想感情。诗人对友人关切爱护，既劝慰友人，又对友人的归隐生活流露出羡慕之情，说明诗人对自己的现实也不很满意。"不得意"三字是理解这首诗题旨的一把钥匙。全诗语言看似平淡无奇，但最后两句却顿增诗意，可谓词浅情深，蕴含着不尽的意味。

At Parting

Dismounted, I drink with you
And ask what you've in view.
"I can't do what I will,
So I'll go to south hill.
Be gone, ask no more, friend,
Let cloud drift without end!"

春夜竹亭赠钱少府归蓝田

夜静群动息[①],
时闻隔林犬。
却忆山中时,
人家涧西远。
羡君明发去,
采蕨轻轩冕[②]。

① 群动息：各种动物停止活动。

② 轩冕：古时大夫以上官员的车乘和冕服，此处借指高官厚禄。

此诗约作于乾元二年（759）春，当时王维任职给事中。钱少府，指钱起，也是著名诗人，王维的朋友，他自乾元二年至宝应二年（763）任职蓝田县尉。这是一首赠别诗，诗人借此表达了自己厌弃俗世纷扰、渴望归隐的愿望。首句，夜深人静，万物都安静了下来，但树林那边的狗还在叫个不停，让人心烦意乱。三、四两句，这扰人的犬吠声，让我想起在辋川别业隐居时的清静日子。在那里，相邻最近的人家也在山涧以西很远的地方，不会像今天这样受吵。尾句，真羡慕你这黎明一去，即可脱离这是非纷扰的京都长安，在蓝田过上那超然世外的隐居生活。

Written on a Spring Night in the Pavilion of Bamboo on Qian Qi's Return to His Blue Field

At night all are quiet and still,
I hear but dogs bark now and then.
I remember life in the hill,
West of the brook, far from all men.
I admire you leaving the court
To gather green herbs long or short.

答张五弟

终南有茅屋,
前对终南山。
终年无客长闭关,
终日无心①长自闲。
不妨饮酒复垂钓,
君但能来相往还②。

① 无心：佛教语，指摆脱了邪念的真心。

② 往还：交往。

张五弟，即张諲，唐代书画家，官至刑部员外郎，因排行第五，故称张五弟。这首小诗表现了诗人在隐居中寂静安闲的生活情趣，又表达了对志趣相投友人的真挚感情。全篇以诗代书，写得朴实、自然、亲切。诗中有意采用重复的字眼和相同的句式。首两句连用两个"终南"，使友人加深印象，突出出门面山的优势。三、四句又巧妙地把终南山的"终"字移用来创造给人以悠长、缓慢之感的时间意象。一个"终年"再叠加一个"终日"，两个同一结构的诗句重复、排比，用以烘托寂寞、清闲的心态，使人感到诗人在山中就这么日复一日、年复一年地静静生活下去，对世事不闻不问，甚至不管岁月的流逝，唯一遗憾的是不能与张諲朝夕相处。

Reply to Cousin Zhang the Fifth

There is my hermitage

By Southern Mountainside.

No guest comes so my door is closed all the age.

I am at leisure all day long unoccupied.

But you may come to drink and fish with me,

If you should like to keep my company.

渭川田家

斜光照墟落①，　　　　　　　① 墟落：村庄。
穷巷②牛羊归。　　　　　　　② 穷巷：深巷。
野老念牧童，
倚杖候荆扉。
雉雊③麦苗秀，　　　　　　　③ 雉(zhì)雊(gòu)：野鸡鸣叫。
蚕眠桑叶稀。
田夫荷④锄至，　　　　　　　④ 荷(hè)：肩扛。
相见语依依。
即此羡闲逸，
怅然吟《式微》。

这首五言古诗当作于开元二十四年（736）张九龄罢相后不久。诗人以白描的艺术手法，生动细致地描摹出一幅充满生活情趣的农家晚归图。诗歌尾句卒章显志，揭示出诗旨所在。《式微》是《诗经·邶风》中的一篇，诗中反复咏叹"式微，式微，胡不归"。诗人此处借用《诗经》句意，抒发了对闲适恬淡的乡村生活的向往，却又身不由己、无法归隐的惆怅之情，不仅在意境上与首句"斜光照墟落"相呼应，而且内容也落在"归"字上，使写景与抒情契合无间、浑然一体。

Rural Scene by River Wei

The village lit by slanting rays,

The cattle trail on homeward ways.

See an old man for the herd wait,

Leaning on staff by wicket gate.

Pheasants call in wheat field with ease;

Silkworms sleep on sparse mulberries.

Shouldering hoe, two ploughmen meet;

They talk long, standing on their feet.

For this unhurried life I long,

Lost in singing "Home-Going Song."

奉①寄韦太守陟

① 奉：敬词。

荒城自萧索，
万里山河空。
天高秋日迥②，
嘹唳③闻归鸿。
寒塘映衰草，
高馆落疏桐。
临此岁方晏④，
顾景⑤咏悲翁。
故人不可见，
寂寞平林东。

② 迥（jiǒng）：远。
③ 嘹唳（lì）：声音响亮凄清。

④ 晏：晚。
⑤ 景（yǐng）：同"影"。

这首诗首联开门见山，直接描写边塞孤城的萧条衰败。这一联中，一"自"一"空"，如神来之笔，画龙点睛。第二联，落笔于高空，秋气肃杀、高远阔大的边城景象。只孤城一座，忽城外几点孤雁，凄厉的鸣叫传入耳际，那是寻找同伴的哀鸣。鸿雁尤可展翅飞翔，而自身呢，便怕要陷身此荒凉之地了，不禁自问何时能归乡。第三联，诗人从身边

For Governor Wei Zhi

The town looks desolate and bleak,

In vain stretch out hill, rill and creek.

The autumn sun sinks from the sky

To hear returning wild geese cry.

The pool is chilled with withered grass,

Sparse plane trees shed their leaves, alas!

It's now near the end of the year,

How can I not sing without cheer!

Oh, where are you, my dear old friend?

Lonely, I see the plain extend.

的细节着眼,眼前池塘凛冽的水,岸边衰败的草,驿馆外稀疏枯干的梧桐,处处如此,又能够向何处逃呢? 第四联,诗人故作刚强,似勉强还能控制住内心无限的惆怅、悲凉。尾联,忽念及自己在这偏远的边塞荒城上,竟无一好友相伴,一时所有的情感如开闸之水,奔涌出来,再也难以控制了。全诗至此,戛然而止,但那难以遣怀的悲愁,却久久不散。

秋夜独坐怀内弟崔兴宗

夜静群动息,
蟪蛄①声悠悠。
庭槐北风响,
日夕方高秋。
思子整羽翮,
及时当云浮。
吾生将白首,
岁晏思沧州。
高足②在旦暮,
肯为南亩俦。

① 蟪(huì)蛄(gū):蝉的一种。

② 高足:此处指代快马。

崔兴宗,王维的内弟,这是作者秋夜独坐,因想念他而作的一首诗。首两句是以动写静、寓静于动的佳句,以"蟪蛄声悠悠"反衬夜的安静。"思子整羽翮,及时当云浮"一句以鸟的振翅欲飞比喻崔兴宗即将出仕。末两句是说,崔兴宗你很快就会高升,将来还会做隐居的朋友吗?夜静而思绪不宁,我静而内弟思动,在对比中显出诗人的无奈、孤单和怅然若失之情。

Thinking of Cousin Cui on an Autumn Night

All living things at night are still,
I only hear cicada's song.
My tree trembles in north wind chill,
Late autumn is coming along.
I think of you flapping your wing
To float like cloud in the sky wide.
A white-haired man would only sing
At the year's end by riverside.
Sooner or later you will fly.
Could I follow you far and nigh?

过李揖宅

闲门秋草色,
终日无车马。
客来深巷中,
犬吠寒林下。
散发时未簪,
道书行尚把。
与我同心人,
乐道安贫者。
一罢宜城酌,
还归洛阳社。

李揖,公元756年为延安太守。首联是说门扉闲闭阶草黄,难见车马来拜访。闲门系指进出往来的人不多,显得清闲的门庭。第二联讲客人自深巷出来,引得寒林里的狗叫起来。寒林系指秋冬的林木,晓霜犹凝,寒风萧瑟,吹得落叶飒飒作响。第三联是说主人李揖为人不羁,出迎时发髻还没簪上,手上拿着《道书》。《道书》是唐代上流社会时行的道家修炼之书。第四联是说李揖与诗人是志同道合的人,安贫乐道地在家乡归隐。尾联是说在李揖宅饮毕美酒,诗人就回归自己的隐居处了。

A Visit to Li Yi's Cottage

Your gate is dyed in autumn grass,

The way untrodden all the day.

Seeing a visitor pass,

The dog in deep forest will bay.

You have not yet pinned up your hair

But come out with your book in hand.

To be rich or poor we don't care,

Our hearts feel same joy in the land.

When we have drunk our cup of wine,

I'll go back to my cottage fine.

送宇文太守赴①宣城

① 赴：这里是赴任的意思。

寥落②云外山，
迢遥③舟中赏。
铙④吹发西江，
秋空多清响。
地迥古城芜，
月明寒潮广。
时赛敬亭神⑤，
复解罟师⑥网。
何处寄相思？
南风吹五两。

② 寥落：稀少，冷落。
③ 迢遥：形容遥远。
④ 铙（náo）：古代军中的乐器。

⑤ 赛敬亭神：旧时的迷信活动。
⑥ 罟（gǔ）师：此处代指渔夫。

公元740年，王维时任殿中侍御史，南进经夏口（今湖北武昌）写了这首五言古诗。这首诗是沿着船行进的路线来写的。前四句是倒写，实际上应是"铙吹发西江，秋空多清响。寥落云外山，迢遥舟中赏"。接下来四句"地迥古城芜，月明寒潮广。时赛敬亭神，复解罟师网"，写诗人已到夏口接近宣城地界看到与想到的。看到的是，古城荒芜，月明清辉，寒潮阵阵；想到的是，宇文太守赴宣城，宣城一定能治理好。最后两句写诗人对宇文太守的思念，表现他与宇文太守的友情。

Seeing Governor Yuwen Off to Xuancheng

Beyond the clouds few mountains stand,
Aboard, you see the far-off land.
On western stream the cymbals blare,
Their echo floats in autumn air.
Different from the drear town old,
The moon shines on tide wide and cold.
Fishermen worship gods with laughter,
And cast their net to catch fish after.
Do you know how fast my longing grows?
See how fast the southern wind blows!

青溪[1]

[1] 青溪：在今陕西勉县之东。

言[2]入黄花川，
每逐青溪水。
随山将万转，
趣[3]途无百里。
声喧乱石中，
色静深松里。
漾漾泛菱荇[4]，
澄澄映葭苇。
我心素已闲，
清川澹[5]如此。
请留盘石上，
垂钓将已矣。

[2] 言：语气词，无义。

[3] 趣：同"趋"，指走过的路途。

[4] 菱(líng)荇(xìng)：水草。

[5] 澹(dàn)：形容溪水澄净。

　　这首诗的题目在《文苑英华》中作《过青溪水作》。青溪名不见经传，就在黄花川。此诗作于诗人入蜀途中。诗人借颂扬名不见经传的青溪，来印证自己的素愿。以青溪之淡泊，喻自身之素愿安闲。诗的每一句都可以独立成为一幅优美的画面，溪流随山势蜿蜒，在乱石中奔腾咆哮，在松林里静静流淌，水面微波荡漾，各种水生植物随波浮动，溪边的巨石上，垂钓老翁消闲自在。诗句自然清淡，绘声绘色，静中有动，托物寄情，韵味无穷。

The Blue Stream

I follow the Blue Rill
To Stream of Yellow Blooms.
It winds from hill to hill
Till far away it looms.
It roars amid pebbles white,
And calms down under pines green.
Weeds float on ripples light,
Reeds mirrored like a screen.
My mind carefree alone,
The clear stream flows with ease.
I would sit on a stone,
To fish whatever I please.

送秘书晁监还日本国

积水不可极，
安知沧海东①！　　　　　　　　① 沧海东：此处代指日本。
九州何处远？
万里若乘空。
向国唯看日，
归帆但信风。
鳌身映天黑，
鱼眼射波红。
乡树扶桑外，
主人孤岛中。
别离方异域，
音信若为通。

这是王维送别诗中又一力作，也是一曲中日两国在唐朝时的友谊之歌。秘书晁监即晁衡，原名阿倍仲麻吕，开元五年（717）以遣唐使来中国，因慕中国之风，留而不去，改名为晁衡。天宝十二载（753），晁衡乘船回国探亲。王维并没有航海的经历，但从目的地的渺远和航程的艰险，诗人声声喟叹，让人感同身受地体会到了航海时的孤独感、神秘感和恐惧感。全诗充满了一种怅惘、忧愁、悬念、惜别等杂糅交织而成的至精至诚的情谊。

Seeing Secretary Chao Back to Japan

The sea is far and wide,

Who knows the other side?

How far is it away?

A thousand miles, you say.

Look at the sun, oh! please.

Your sail should trust the breeze.

Turtles bear the dark sky;

Giant fishes raise waves high.

When you are in your isle,

There're trees from mile to mile.

Though we're separated for long,

Would you send me your song?

晓行巴峡

际晓①投巴峡,　　　　　　　　①际晓：黎明。
余春忆帝京。
晴江一女浣,
朝日众鸡鸣。
水国舟中市,
山桥树杪②行。　　　　　　　　②树杪(miǎo)：树梢。
登高万井③出,　　　　　　　　③万井：此处代指千家万户。
眺迥二流明。
人作殊方④语,　　　　　　　　④殊方：远方，异域。
莺为故国声。
赖多山水趣,
稍解别离情。

巴峡，长江自巴县（今四川重庆）至涪州（今四川涪陵）一段有明月、黄葛、铜锣、石洞、鸡鸣、黄草等峡，这些峡皆在古巴县或巴郡境内，因统称为巴峡。本诗描写了巴峡周围的景色和风土人情。词句清丽，景象雄伟。水国舟市，道尽水乡的独特风貌；桥过树梢，极写山乡的奇幻景观。"登高万井出，眺迥二流明"，使人视野开阔，诗歌意境也随之宏远。不同的方言俚俗，相同的莺啼鸟叫，写尽在外流浪漂泊的异乡人的思念之情。此地虽有山水情趣，也只能稍事排解离别之情、思念之苦。

Passing Through the Gorge in the Morning

Our boat enters the Western Gorge at dawn,
Unlike the capital in vernal morn.
A maiden washes her things by the stream;
All roasters crow to welcome the sunbeam.
People bargain in the boat as they please;
The arching bridge seems higher than the trees.
All village huts emerge when you climb high;
When you look far, two clear rivers flow by.
With a strange accent people talk along,
But southern orioles too sing northern song.
By luck the delights of mountains and streams
Will alleviate my homesickness in dreams.

西施咏

艳色天下重,
西施宁久微?
朝为越溪女,
暮作吴宫妃。
贱日岂殊众①?　　　　　　　　　　①殊众:不同于众,出众。
贵来方悟稀。
邀人傅脂粉,
不自着罗衣。
君宠益娇态,
君怜无是非。
当②时浣纱伴,　　　　　　　　　　②当:又写作"常"。
莫得同车归。
持谢③邻家子,　　　　　　　　　　③持谢:奉告。
效颦安可希!

本诗取材于历史人物,借古讽今。诗的开首四句写西施有艳丽的姿色,终不能久处低微。诗人借西施"朝贱夕贵"而浣纱同伴中仅她一人命运发生改变的经历,感叹世态炎凉,抒发怀才不遇的不平与感慨。诗的次六句写西施一旦得到君王宠爱,就身价百倍。诗人借世人只见显贵时的西施之美,表达对势利小人的嘲讽。诗人借"朝为越溪女"的西施

Song of the Beauty of the West

A beauty is loved far and wide.
How could she be unknown for long?
At dawn she washed by riverside;
At dusk to the king she'll belong.
Poor, she was one of lower race;
Ennobled, she's one of the few.
She has maids to powder her face
And dress her up with silk dress new.
Royal favor adds to her charms;
Royal love turns wrong into right.
Her companions wash with bare arms,
Could they attain such royal height?
To washerwomen I would say:
Don't follow her unusual way!

"暮作吴宫妃"后的骄纵，讥讽那些由于偶然机遇受到恩宠就趾高气扬、不可一世的人。诗歌最后四句写姿色太差的人，想效颦西施是不自量力。诗人借效颦的东施，劝告世人不要为了博取别人赏识而故作姿态，弄巧成拙。语虽浅显，寓意深刻。沈德潜在《唐诗别裁集》中说："写尽炎凉人眼界，不为题缚，乃臻斯诣。"

田 园 乐

（七首其二）

再见封侯万户，
立谈①赐璧一双。
讵②胜耦③耕南亩，
何如高卧东窗！

① 立谈：在交谈的当时。

② 讵（jù）：难道。表反问。

③ 耦（ǒu）：两个人在一起耕地。

《田园乐》是王维的一组七首六言绝句，本书选了其中六首。该组诗为作者退隐辋川时所作，故一题作《辋川六言》。这首诗的前两句所用典故见《史记·平原君虞卿列传》，说的是虞卿游说赵孝成王，立谈而封侯，一见赐黄金百镒、白璧一双，再见为赵上卿。此处用典意在说明顷刻间即致富贵。全诗的主旨就是即使像虞卿一样立谈而封侯，也不如像长沮、桀溺一样躬耕自给，过着隐者闲适的生活。

Seven Idylls

(II)

I would not be ennobled lord,
Nor favored with a pair of jade.
I'll till the field I can afford,
And lie on the couch in the shade.

田 园 乐

（七首其三）

采菱渡头风急，
策杖①林西日斜。　　　　　① 策杖：拄着棍杖。
杏树坛边渔父，
桃花源里人家。

关于《辋川六言》，顾璘曰：首首如画。此首亦是如此。策杖即扶杖之意。"杏树坛边渔父"用典见《庄子·渔父》：孔子弦歌，鼓琴奏曲未半，有渔父下船而来，须眉交白，被发揄袂，行原以上，距陆而止，左手据膝，右手持颐以听。意指此地有能听琴的高雅渔父。可以想象诗人过着"渡头采菱迎风急""策杖于山林观日落"的如仙境般的桃源生活，又能在杏林坛边遇到知音，人生如此，夫复何求。

Seven Idylls

(III)

I'd gather chestnuts in the breeze
And see the sun sink, cane in hand.
A fisherman amid the trees
Hears the sage in Peach Blossom Land.

田 园 乐

（七首其四）

萋萋芳草春绿，
落①落长松夏寒。　　　　　　　① 落：树木高大的样子。
牛羊自归村巷，
童稚不识衣冠②。　　　　　　　② 衣冠：士大夫的穿着打扮。

　　以"萋萋"来形容芳草丰茂，以"落落"来形容松树高盛。萋萋芳草带给春天的是一片鲜绿，落落长松带给夏天的是阴凉风爽。这个"寒"字看似无理，用在此处极为精妙。牛羊也无需牧人，自己就能在放牧之后回到村庄。村里的顽童哪里认得什么身着官衣的士大夫。这样蔑视权贵、闲适安逸的山林田园生活，不正是诗人一贯的精神追求吗？

Seven Idylls

(IV)

Luxuriant grass will turn the season green,
And shady pines would cool the summer day.
Children cannot tell the rich from the mean;
The cattle go their backward way.

田 园 乐

（七首其五）

山下孤烟远村，

天边独树高原。

一瓢颜回①陋巷，

五柳先生②对门。

① 颜回：即颜渊。

② 五柳先生：陶渊明的别称。

这首诗像一幅萧疏清淡的水墨画，山下与天边相呼应，就更可见其远。孤烟与独树相呼应，更衬托出人烟非常稀少。远村与高原相呼应，就更令人感到苍凉孤寂。这两句在画面上，色彩极为淡薄，可以看到那远处孤烟尚带一缕淡灰，那天边高原似有一层淡黄。在此清静的天地中，有颜回、陶潜那样的雅兴，多么恬适安闲、自由自在。倘若没有淡到极致的修养，则不能臻此妙境。如果说前两句是重在描绘冲淡的景物，那么后两句是重在抒发冲淡的情感。而冲淡的景情，又是彼此交融、相互渗透的。

Seven Idylls

(V)

A wreath of smoke rises from far away,
On the horizon stands a lonely tree.
A sage may live in shabby lane all day;
Under five willows a hermit is free.

田园乐

(七首其六)

桃红复含宿雨,
柳绿更带春烟[①]。
花落家童[②]未扫,
莺啼山客犹眠。

① 春烟:春天里因气候变暖而产生的烟雾。
② 家童:家中的仆人。

    春桃更带雨润,分外妖娆动人。绿柳掩映于春烟,自见其婀娜之风姿。花落处恰是满园春色,家童未及收扫,更带出了一番春天悠然之风韵。有前三句的映衬,主人飘逸之神情于莺啼酣眠之际呼之欲出。桃是妖娆,柳是嫩绿,花是满园,莺是陪侍,此一番景致,真乃天上人间耳。此时此刻,此事此景才是诗佛王维心中真正之归宿,由是才能酣然而眠。

Seven Idylls

(VI)

Peach flowers reddened by night rain,
Green willows veiled in mist of spring.
The fallen blooms unswept remain;
The hermit sleeps when orioles sing.

田 园 乐

（七首其七）

酌酒会临泉水，
抱琴好倚长松。
南园露葵①朝折，
东谷黄粱夜舂②。

① 露葵：莼菜。
② 舂：把东西放在石臼或乳钵里捣掉皮和壳或捣碎。

    泉边饮酒，松下弹琴，这正是诗人所向往的隐者神仙般的生活。然而这种隐者生活也离不开朝折露葵，夜舂黄粱的人间生活，正是所谓的天上人间，表现出诗人隐居生活的情趣。六言体诗歌上下两句常常是对仗工整，互增意趣。与刘长卿的六言体八句一体不同，王维的六言体往往是四句一体。

Seven Idylls

(VII)

By fountainside I drink my wine
And play my lute, leaning on pine.
Plucking sunflowers in twilight,
I pound eastern millet at night.

陇头吟

长安少年游侠客,
夜上戍楼看太白。
陇头明月迥临关,
陇上行人①夜吹笛。
关西老将不胜愁,
驻马听之双泪流。
身经大小百余战,
麾下偏裨②万户侯。
苏武才为典属国,
节旄③落尽海西头。

① 行人:出征的人。
② 偏裨(pí):偏将,裨将。将佐的通称。
③ 节旄(máo):旌节上所缀的牦牛尾饰物。

  这是王维用乐府旧题写的一首著名边塞诗,题目一作"边情"。"陇头吟"即"陇头",汉代乐府曲辞名,属横吹曲辞,李延年造。陇头,指陇山一带,大致在今陕西陇县至甘肃平凉一带。本诗写到"长安少年""陇上行人""关西老将"这三个人物,其中关西老将又引苏武与之类比,表面似乎是安慰关西老将,实际上恰恰说明了关西老将的遭遇不是偶然的。功大赏小,功小赏大,朝廷不公,古来如此,从而深化了诗的主题。而今日的长安少年,安知不是明日的陇上行人,后日的关西老将?而今日的关西老将,又安知不是昨日的陇上行人,前日的长安少年?诗的主旨是发人深省的。

A Frontier Song

A hero of the capital comes from afar,
He mounts the tower to watch the evening star.
The moon shines bright on city walls of the frontier;
The wayfarer at night plays his flute sad and drear.
A sorrow-laden general stops his steed and hears,
But how could he stop his two flowing streams of tears!
He's hardened by hundreds of battles far and nigh;
Officers under him are promoted to posts high.
He's still in charge of the border's petty affairs,
Like an old shepherd by the seaside no one cares.

桃源行

渔舟逐水①爱山春，
两岸桃花夹古津。
坐②看红树不知远，
行尽青溪不见人。
山口潜行始隈③隩，
山开旷望旋④平陆。
遥看一处攒云树，
近入千家散花竹。
樵客初传汉姓名，
居人未改秦衣服。
居人共住武陵源，
还从物外起田园。
月明松下房栊⑤静，
日出云中鸡犬喧。

① 逐水：顺着溪水。

② 坐：因为。

③ 隈（wēi）：山脉弯曲，水流拐弯的地方。

④ 旋：不久。

⑤ 房栊（lóng）：房屋的窗户。

这是王维19岁时写的一首七言乐府诗，本诗以陶渊明的《桃花源记》为蓝本，取其大意，变文为诗，进行了艺术的再创造，开拓了诗的意境，具有独特的艺术价值。因而本诗能与散文《桃花源记》并传于世。《桃花源记》描写的是与世隔绝的"人境"，本诗写的是"仙境"。王维以理想的田园环

Song of Peach Blossom Land

A fisherman loved vernal hills and winding stream,
His boat between the shores, he saw peach blossoms beam.
He knew not how far he'd gone, charmed by blooming scene,
Up to the end of the stream not a man was seen.
At the foot of the hill he found a winding way,
Beyond the hills a plain extended far, far away.
Viewed from afar, the forest seemed to scrape the sky;
Bamboos and flowers scattered in houses nearby.
A woodman told him a name used long, long ago,
People were dressed in a style now no one would know.
As they had lived together in Peach Blossom Land,
Beyond the bustle fields were tilled with plough in hand.
Under moonlit pines cots looked quiet in the dark,
Up to sunlit clouds cocks crow was heard with dogs' bark.

境来刻画桃源仙境,这种仙凡一体的艺术手法在盛唐诗歌中具有代表性。清人王士禛说:"唐宋以来,作《桃源行》最佳者,王摩诘(维)、韩退之(愈)、王介甫(安石)三篇。观退之、介甫二诗,笔力意思甚可喜。及读摩诘诗,多少自在;二公便如努力挽强,不免面红耳热,此盛唐所以高不可及。"

惊闻俗客争来集,
竞引还家问都邑。
平明闾巷扫花开,
薄暮渔樵乘水入。
初因避地去人间,
及至成仙遂不还。
峡里谁知有人事?
世中遥望空云山。
不疑灵境难闻见,
尘心未尽思乡县。
出洞无论隔山水,
辞家终拟长游衍①。

① 游衍:流连忘返。

自谓经过旧不迷,
安知峰壑今来变。
当时只记入山深,
青溪几度到云林?
春来遍是桃花水,
不辨仙源何处寻。

Curious about the stranger, they came from up and down,
Led him to their cottages and asked about the town.
Fallen petals on the lane were swept clean by day,
At dusk fishermen and woodmen on homeward way.
Their fathers left the war-torn land to flee from woe,
This fairyland was found, away they would not go.
Deep in the vale, no one cared about world affair;
Gazing afar, they longed for cloud and mountain air.
Knowing not such fairyland was hard to be refound,
The fisherman longed to go back to his native ground.
He left the place and passed over mountains and streams,
But how could he forget the scene of his dear dreams?
He thought, having come once, he would not go astray,
Without knowing peak and stream would change on the way.
Last time he came, he only knew the mountain deep,
But memory of cloudy way he did not keep.
When spring came, everywhere he saw peach blossoms nice.
But where could he find again his lost paradise!

图书在版编目（CIP）数据

许渊冲译王维诗选：汉文，英文 /（唐）王维著；许渊冲编译. -- 北京：中译出版社，2021.1（2022.7重印）
（许渊冲英译作品）
ISBN 978-7-5001-6452-4

Ⅰ.①许… Ⅱ.①王… ②许… Ⅲ.①唐诗－诗集－汉、英 Ⅳ.①I222.742

中国版本图书馆CIP数据核字（2020）第240383号

出版发行	中译出版社
地　　址	北京市西城区新街口外大街28号普天德胜大厦主楼4层
电　　话	(010)68359719
邮　　编	100088
电子邮箱	book@ctph.com.cn
网　　址	http://www.ctph.com.cn

出 版 人	乔卫兵
总 策 划	刘永淳
责任编辑	刘香玲　张　旭
文字编辑	王秋璎　张莞嘉　赵浠彤
营销编辑	毕竞方

赏　　析	李旻
封面制作	刘哲
内文制作	黄浩　北京竹页文化传媒有限公司
印　　刷	天津新华印务有限公司
经　　销	新华书店

规　　格	840mm×1092mm　1/32
印　　张	6.875
字　　数	224千
版　　次	2021年1月第1版
印　　次	2022年7月第6次

ISBN 978-7-5001-6452-4　定价：46.00元

版权所有　侵权必究
中译出版社